TROUBLE

TROUBLE

Published by University of Huddersfield Press

University of Huddersfield Press
The University of Huddersfield
Queensgate
Huddersfield HD1 3DH
Email enquiries university.press@hud.ac.uk

First published 2019
Text © 2019 all named authors and Editor Simon Crump.

This work is licensed under a Creative Commons Attribution 4.0 International License
Images © as attributed

Every effort has been made to locate copyright
holders of materials included and to obtain
permission for their publication.

The publisher is not responsible for the continued
existence and accuracy of websites referenced
in the text.

All rights reserved. No part of this book may be
reproduced in any form or by any means without
prior permission from the publisher.

A CIP catalogue record for this book is available
from the British Library.
ISBN 978-1-86218-158-8
e-ISBN 978-1-86218-159-5
Designed by Carnegie Book Production
Printed by Amadeus Press
COVER IMAGE: Photo by Oladimeji Odunsi on Unsplash

Contents

Editorial Team	vii
Introduction	ix
The Flag 　Mary Fox	1
You and Me in Paradise 　Martin Nathan	7
The Walk of Blood 　M. A. Hodgson	21
The Unplayable 　Bruce Harris	25
Meet, me. 　Bex O'Gorman	38
Mr Laurence and Numb Nuts 　Ledlowe Guthrie	48
Of Love and Revolution in a City 　Tabitha Bast	55
Happy Harpies 　Miriam Burke	61
Boots 　Elizabeth Woodgate	68

Three Conversations with Mr Sienkiewicz Jonathan Holland	73
A Haunting A. B. G. Murray	86
But Have You Seen it In the Snow? Tabitha Bast	87
Losing Control Matt Hill	92
Last of Them Aaron Haviland	101
You will be free one day, my dearest India. Sarah Hussain	110
The Only Language She Didn't Understand Robert Kibble	117
The Most Dangerous Woman Martin Nathan	122
Nachthexan Jim Lewis	133
A State of Grace Bud Craig	137
Money Bank Bethany Ridley-Duff	151
The Calling Michael Bird	162
About the Authors	173
About Grist	178
Acknowledgements	178

EDITORIAL TEAM

Caitlin Bastow
Liam Crew
Jonathan Croft
Simon Crump
Lottie Edwards
Beth Greenhalgh
Charlotte Rhodes
Beth Ridley-Duff
Georgia Turner-Beach

INTRODUCTION

At 1.25pm on 2nd November 2016 I was arrested with fellow tree protester Calvin Payne on Marden Road, Sheffield for trying to prevent the felling of a hundred year old street tree which was perfectly healthy and still very much in its prime. We were taken away in a police van and locked in the cells at Shepcote Lane Detention Suite for over eight hours. We were questioned, photographed, fingerprinted and DNA swabs were taken. We were charged with breaking an obscure anti-Trade Union law and released. Two days later, a court date arrived in the post. We attended court to plead not guilty and the charges were subsequently dropped as not being in the Public Interest. Since then I have been arrested again (and again the charges were dropped for the same reason), I am currently the subject of a High Court injunction and I have a suspended prison sentence. All for peacefully protesting against the needless felling of thousands of perfectly healthy Sheffield street trees.

My experience on the ground in Sheffield is being echoed across the country. Local and national government is being sold off to private companies, and when that happens the public's right to have a say is often lost in the world of PFI commercial contracts. Sometimes protest is the only option left available to us.

Protest is the distillation of a simple human experience: to see a wrong being done and, on a very basic level, to try to do something about it. In my role as the editor of Grist it seems appropriate that our new anthology should reflect what has become a significant part of my life. With the rise of the anti-fracking movement, of Extinction Rebellion, of Youth Strike 4 Climate, and an increasing disillusionment with the existing political system, protest appears to be our last best hope as we tumble headlong into the anthropocene.

The stories featured here in the 2019 Grist anthology *Trouble* celebrate protest, rebellion, disobedience and general bloody-mindedness in all of its forms. The pen is no longer mightier than the sword sadly, but when the shouting stops, that's when the writing begins to do its job.

The best writing about protest should inspire, educate, motivate, compel and of course, entertain. And that's what this collection is all about. There are historical protest stories here – *The Flag, Happy Harpies* – stories set in the future – *Money Bank, Last of Them* – stories of personal protest against sexual and racial discrimination – *Meet Me, The Walk of Blood* – and the closing story, *The Calling,* which embodies the simple truth that sometimes all you can do in protest is to make a lot of noise.

Simon Crump

Persons Unknown: The Battle for Sheffield's Street Trees by Simon Crump and Calvin Payne, with be published by University of Huddersfield Press in 2020

The Flag
MARY FOX

I folded the return train ticket inside my purse and then pushed that inside the satchel strapped across my shoulder. Tucking the green and purple flag as deep into the outside pocket as it would go, I stepped down onto the platform. The steam hissed as the pistons slowly pushed the train away from the station. It was a glorious first Saturday in June.

The throng was so dense as I crossed the course at Tattenham Corner that at times I was swept from my feet and, not being very strong, carried through the air by this shoal of wild excited men crushed together, maybe thirty deep. We squeezed through the gap in the railings and then, like water forced from a gulley, sprayed hither and thither across the vast downs.

'Lucky heather, lady?' She thrust a sprig wrapped in tissue with a punch into my chest. The nails were black, the skin as creased and brown as any I had seen before. Next to her, on a fence post, two magpies hopped and cawed, heads cocked sideways. I felt inside my bodice and touched my mother's letter. The gypsy looked me up and down and retracted her offering perhaps realising that I needed more than good luck today.

I moved easily amidst the crowd. I had chosen my darkest dress coat with my bonnet pulled down low so that people might not even guess I was a woman. I had an hour to wait for the last race, so I took the chance to look around.

A section of the grass inside the course was roped off for a fair. Children screamed as they galloped around a track on painted iron horses. A man on stilts proffered toffee apples to an infant but she bawled in terror. One little girl had her head thrown back, her little body almost paralysed with joy. She reminded me of my own sweet niece and the sadness weighed down on me suddenly, with surprising force. I often felt dizzy these days. My leg had never straightened properly and several of my vertebrae had fused together after I threw myself down the stairs at Holloway. I leant against a post for a moment, breathing deeply to work against the pain that throbbed through my spine.

I took the letter out from my bodice. It was now as soft as calf skin where it had been opened so many times. It read:

My darling Em.
I hope I find you well. It has turned out to be a glorious summer in Morpeth after all. Spring was late coming here this year but now the garden is resplendent with hollyhocks and even the tea-rose you sent me is starting to bloom in Fox Corner. I hope this letter arrives before you go to the Derby in June. Please be careful, my darling Em. I know how impulsive you are and the races attract all sorts of disreputable people.

Also, sweet Em, I had the most disconcerting experience only two days ago. I was just looking out of the kitchen window admiring the garden, when a single magpie landed on the sill. I banged on the glass to shoo it away. But it would not move so I opened the kitchen door and in it flew. I had to chase the terrified thing around, trying to liberate it. In its panic it just flapped and slapped into things, causing the most horrible mess with feathers and excrement everywhere. Finally, it flew up into the chimney breast and disappeared.

I feel it is the most terrible omen, Em. So please be careful. Your fall at Holloway caused me so much heartache and I thought I would lose you then. I know you are so devoted to 'the Cause' and I love your dedication but please try to rest, dearest Em, so your back may heal a little.

I look forward to seeing you later in the summer. We can sit in the garden and drink lemonade and look at the flowers.

Take good care now and God bless you,
Your loving mother.

I sniffed the lavender-infused pages of the letter. Oh Mother, if only you were here with me now. I looked down from my vantage point at the top of the hill. There were many tic-tac men standing on their boxes in the valley at the bottom. Some were in caps, some bare-headed. Some shouted their odds to their comrades. Others gesticulated wildly, tapping their noses and patting the top of their heads. I felt a sudden irrational compulsion to place a bet and walked down to where the men stood. A kindly faced man, with a pencil behind his ear and a notebook in his hand, looked down at me.

'I'll put two shillings on Aboyeur,' I called up to him. He gave me the ticket. To my right-hand side a man in a bowler hat sniggered.

'Aboyeur is the outsider, madam. You'll be wasting your money.' He spoke in an annoying cockney accent heavily laced with hints of faux sophistication and wore his bowler pulled down over greying sideburns. Although the comment was addressed to me he turned to smile at the girl clinging to his arm. She was a small wisp of a thing with white, translucent skin and watery blue eyes. She had far too much makeup on and beneath the pan I could see she had probably not yet reached her seventeenth birthday. She simpered and giggled. He looked down at my purse noticing the green and purple flag sticking out of it. His face darkened.

'So, this is how you lot waste your time is it? Betting on the horses? Shouldn't you be chained to a railing or throwing rocks at the prime minister you dirty whore?' He hissed and then pointed at me. 'Look here,' he shouted to the crowd, 'a filthy suffragette.'

I felt the fear rise up to my throat and my legs moved as though through aspic, but I walked briskly away and tried to lose myself in the throng. Did I really have the stomach for this? I had always thought I was strong enough and yet maybe I misunderstood what strength was. I prayed the courage would come from somewhere when I needed it most.

Ahead stood a group of three plain tents, the only visible shelter I could spot. I ducked in under the flap, hoping to hide from the crowd. It smelt strongly of carbolic soap inside.

'Oh, a lady visitor. That's new. Clean yourself up Minnie.'

In the corner of the tent a wan-faced girl was squatting over a bucket cleaning between her legs with a rag. She hummed to herself as she performed her ablutions, rapt in a reverie of her own.

'Are you lookin' for company?' the girl's mother laughed. 'We do get ladies lookin'. We are happy to accommodate all.'

She made a grand sweep with her arm. 'It's a crown for a half hour.' She grinned again, pleased with her own largesse.

'Oh no. I was just interested in what you were doing.'

'Oh. That's my Min. She provides the services. Poor Min's not got the brains she were born with so I look after his lordship.'

I then realised that the woollen sack in her lap was her grandson: a baby with a face as puce as the knitted suit he was wearing.

'He can scream like a lord can't he?' And with that she unleashed a massive breast from its bodice and stuffed it into the bawling face. I placed a crown in the older lady's palm and covered her hand tight around it.

'Please give it to the girl so she can buy the baby a toy,' I stammered, suddenly ashamed of my full purse. Poor simple Minnie. I could only thank God that she was unaware of the wretchedness of her situation.

The grandmother threw her head back and laughed and I could see that her jaw was almost as toothless as that of the baby suckling at her breast.

'A toy eh? Some bread would be more bleedin' use.' I lifted the flap to leave and checked the man in the bowler was nowhere to be seen.

'If you can wait a while lovey, she'll be clean in a minute...'

Glad for the sweet air, I returned to the crowd with the buzz of Minnie's humming still fresh in my head. Should I have said something to her? Tried to persuade her there was a better way than this? Offered her and her son a home for as long as she needed? But I did none of those things and by being silent, I had colluded. What would happen to her? Now I felt small and very empty like the eye of a storm passing dully through the surrounding chaos.

There was no sign of the man in the bowler hat or his young companion. I chose a hillock close to the children's enclosure. It afforded me a clear view from Tattenham Corner to the finishing line. Even the steam from the roast chestnut handcart could not obscure the spectacular panorama. From this vantage point the truth assailed me: apart from a few crumpled mothers the only women here were whores, beggars and mistresses. And myself of course, who, as my mother often joked, was always impossible to categorise.

Feeling ravenously hungry, as though I had been scooped out inside, I planted myself down in the midst of the madness on the first bare patch of grass I could see. My coat pockets were deep and I unwrapped a twist of salt, a hard-boiled egg, a slice of corned beef and some yellow plums from the orchard. A man sitting on his own watched all the while. He had an annoying twinkle in his eye and doffed his hat. I felt the gaze weigh down on me like a hot brand and turned my back to him. But I knew he continued to watch and felt the shadow of his approach until he formed a dark pool all around me.

'Did you enjoy your picnic?' I pretended not to hear him. 'I should think you did. I never thought I would envy a plum.' He tapped his cane next to me.

'Look, go away will you?' I shaded my face with my hand and stared up at him.

'I can show you something tastier than that old plum. What do you say?' I turned away, aware of a burning flush rising up from my throat. I felt so angry I could spit.

'Look. Go away. Please.' I hissed and stepped back into the shadow, clutching the flag in two white-knuckled claws, holding it out in front of me as though for protection. My hands were shaking – partly in fear, but mainly in anger. From the corner of my eye I saw his face harden as he noticed the green and purple flag and I felt the sharp tap on my back from his cane.

'Dirty suffrage pig,' he whispered, and disappeared into the throng.

At that moment, my veins contracted. I felt firework-angry, seething just below my skin, ready to be set off. But I knew I could not respond: not today. I had other work to do. At that moment, a cheer went up from the crowd. A man with a megaphone announced the start of the race, 'Ladies and Gentlemen. Please place your final bets. The Derby will begin in five minutes' time. Last call for betting, please. Last call.' My heart felt as though it would bolt through my chest. I steadied myself and breathed deeply. Should I go back? Oh Mother, help me now. I looked over my shoulder, but the crowd had closed in behind me. No, there was no way back. Forward then.

And in that very moment, just before I stepped out, a kind of ecstasy engulfed me. The same exhilaration I had felt at Holloway the second before I jumped. For although I had known then that the ending would be terrible, I had no control over the moment. I could not stop it. And so it was now. I felt a strange peace, a quietening of the heart, a softening of the limbs. Onward then.

I pushed my way towards the barrier. I made sure I had a good view of the approach to Tattenham corner from where I was standing. I squeezed under it by the side of the course.

'Oi. We're all trying to get a good view,' somebody shouted at me, but I could barely hear with the thunder of hooves approaching and loudest of all, the pumping of blood around my ears and skull.

I stepped out and the first group thundered by. Bunched together in one mass of chestnut flesh and legs flailing and flashes of silk. I was rooted. So close, that clods of earth and dust rained down upon my bonnet and apron. I was baptised with the fat globs of sweat that sprayed from the beautiful beasts and one speck of blood, from the whip of the jockey in gold, struck me on the cheek. The back rider turned to scream a warning to the oncoming horses. Faces contorted into masks of howling confusion, the profanities hailed down upon my head as they swerved by me. One even tried to whip me as he passed.

I stepped forward towards the middle of the course. The roars were deafening as the last beast hurtled towards me. Every vein throbbed through the flesh. The coat shone with a patina of sweat. I could see every sinew of the jockey's twisted jaw. Man and beast locked in magnificent rhythm. I had the flag in my hand and reached up. A flutter of black and white swooped low, obscuring the blinding sun for a moment.

And then they were upon me.

You and Me in Paradise
MARTIN NATHAN

For the comfort and convenience of our guests and the smooth running of the building, we request that residents do not offer gratuities to staff, or discuss personal matters with them.

The concierge led Mark into the apartment, pointing out the fine marble floor, the air-conditioning controls; he demonstrated the television, flicking through pages of channels, Arabic, African, European. He showed him the double sinks with taps, whose operation required such a fleeting touch as to be practically psychic and how to adjust the lights in brightness and hue to match every conceivable mood.

'Even extreme rage?' said Mark.

The concierge allowed his thin moustache to crease in a smile to acknowledge his guest's little joke, and he finished by saying, 'Whatever we can do to help, is our pleasure,' in a hushed reverent tone. He lifted the apartment brochure with its slogan, 'Perfect service, imperceptibly,' in florid gold script, passing his hand over the words to absorb their magic.

'There is just one thing. I'd like to be able to open the window.'

The concierge's smile did not change as Mark attempted to manipulate the window catches, but they remained firmly locked.

The concierge headed to the air conditioning controls. 'This system regulates the atmosphere to your exact requirement. Hot or cold as you like. Filtered quality air. Let me show you again.'

'I would like to open the window.'

'The air outside is not good. But I will make a note of your request.'

'Thank you. Will it take long?'

'I will do it straight away.'

'No, but how long to unlock the windows?'

The concierge was smiling. 'As I said, your request will be actioned promptly.' He closed his eyes, breathing deeply. 'Perfectly regulated.'

Mark looked out of the window onto the area below, with its polished concrete dyed into geometric patterns, creating a path heading towards the mall with its green copper minarets. Receding into the distance, towers were in various stages of construction, each one populated by hundreds of migrant workers crawling around the skeletons of the upper storeys, wearing uniforms of orange and white.

He had come to work at site on the east of the city, a complex of luxury flats and leisure facilities. He had decided to look for work abroad after returning to find his Crystal Palace flat emptied of his wife's clothes. He had sat in the kitchen surrounded by the boxes of the units he'd spent months trying to assemble, with her note that it took him three days to read.

He had been candid in the job agency. 'I'm not sure I'm really qualified for this.'

The agent persuaded him that it was his doubts that showed he was the ideal candidate for the job. 'Safety Adviser. It's common sense. You read their safety documents. If they're okay you sign them off. If not, you don't.'

'So when do I have an interview?'

The agent had smiled. 'That was it.'

They paid for his flight and as he arrived at the airport, the brief blast of the baking air stopped him, breathless. He looked up at a poster of a man of an uncertain ethnicity smiling at his jewelled sports watch. Underneath was the slogan, 'Everything is possible.'

He requested his driver take him straight to site from the airport, but instead found himself delivered to the apartment, where the site manager greeted him with a long handshake and sweet mint tea. The site manager expressed horror at Mark's plan to start work straight away.

'Rest. Explore…'

'I'm not just going to sign a report, you know. I want to do site inspections.'

Despite his sleek grey suit, the site manager clutched a pristine hard-hat and gloves. He was always ready for action. 'Of course not,' he said. 'You must see everything. Tomorrow.'

Mark suggested that accommodation closer to the work site might be better. Unfortunately, nothing was available with a suitable level of comfort.

'A driver will collect you every day. Anywhere you want to go.'

'I'll make my own way.'

'That is not possible. You would die.'

Later Mark walked a circuit of the outside of his apartment block. Even that was very difficult.

The whole block seemed barely occupied. If he heard footsteps, or caught sight of someone, they had always disappeared before an encounter occurred. Despite the newness, one of the bathroom taps dripped. With the perfect condition of everything else it began to obsess him. He phoned the concierge.

'Of course, sir. Right away.'

A few minutes later a young Indian man in a boiler suit arrived carrying a toolbox and an enthusiastic smile. 'Sir. No problem, sir,' he said, disappearing into the bathroom. There was banging.

'All finished,' he said, still smiling.

'Thank you.'

'No problem, sir.'

'Where are you from?'

The man looked puzzled. 'From downstairs.'

'No, are you from India? Whereabouts in India?'

The man passed his hand over the tap and water flowed. He spoke softly. 'Kerala, sir. Lot of water in Kerala.' He demonstrated the tap once more and as he headed towards the door to leave, his face turned wistful.

Mark held out his hand. 'I'm Mark. Thank you.'

The man hesitated, looking at the hand suspiciously, before shaking it. 'What is your name?'

'Arshad. Arshad Kamal.'

'Just one more thing Arshad… The window… do you have something to open the window?'

Arshad pointed to the concierge button on the phone. 'That button, sir. To report.'

In the morning Mark's car didn't turn up, and when he rang site, they told him it had been outside waiting for him. 'But he didn't call me to say he was there.'

'He is there when you need him. I will send him back for you, sir.'

'Thanks. He will call when he arrives?'

When Mark called back later they said the driver had again waited downstairs but had now been called away. The driver would return shortly.

Mark waited in the lobby, flicking through site reports, sitting next to a petrified tree.

At last the car returned.

'Journey… how long?' He gestured a steering motion to the driver.

'One hour.' He smiled. 'Site close in one hour. Work finish.'

'Tomorrow. Early start. Call.' He gave the driver a slip with his mobile number on it.

Mark got out of the car and took the site reports back to his room.

'He will be there. Whenever you require,' the office told him when he rang to explain.

The apartment was serviced, with a pristine and minimal kitchen. The basement restaurant could provide a range of cuisines at any time of day, but Mark decided to visit the mall to buy food to prepare himself.

He smiled at the concierge on the front desk, and followed the covered way to the tiled entrance. 'The Gateway to Paradise' it said in golden letters. He wandered round the circuit with a family group that consisted of a veiled woman in a voluminous gown, a stocky adolescent boy with a skateboard, and a line of girls, time-lapsed through adolescent years. They glanced indifferently into each outlet, and the staff gazed back with even less interest.

He discovered luxury goods, electronics, perfumes and western-branded clothes, but nowhere that sold food. He stopped at a music shop to look at an oud on a stand, fascinated by the deep sheen of the polished wood, the decorated sound hole, the fluting of the tuning pegs. He wanted it.

The assistant came over, shaking his head. 'Not for you,' he said. 'Not for English. Arab. Arab music.' He steered him towards electric guitars.

Mark was going to argue but realised he would have to try the instrument in the shop with the sales assistants listening and watching. 'Not for English.' Mark bought a CD of oud music instead.

'Welcome back sir.' The concierge greeted him as if he was returning from an epic trip of endurance rather than a twenty-minute stroll round the mall.

He sensed something had changed in his apartment. The previous evening he had rearranged the furniture, moving the sofa towards the window and putting the chair back in the corner to create a bigger space, but now they had begun a journey back towards their original positions.

The tap was dripping again.

'Kerala is a beautiful place. I visited once,' he said to the young handyman as he arrived to fix the tap again.

'This country, very beautiful. Good work. Lot of work. Best place.'

'No but Kerala… you must miss it.'

Arshad shrugged.

Mark pointed to a roll of blue tape in Arshad's toolbox. 'Can I have it?' He unpeeled a note from his wallet.

Arshad smiled as Mark tucked the money into the pocket of his overalls. 'No sir,' he said shaking his head, without attempting to return it.

'Any news on the window Arshad?' Mark unpeeled another note.

Arshad patted the money inside his pocket. 'This. Beautiful country. Kerala, no work.' He pointed to the concierge button on the wall-phone. 'Window.'

'Do you send money home to your family?' Mark put pieces of blue tape on the marble to mark the positions of the sofa and chairs.

When it got dark, Mark went outside to the rear of the building and lay on the concrete far below his window, which still retained the heat as if he was in the embers of a fire. He stared up at the sky and its haze flashed with the lights of a distant nightclub. Bass-beats thudded through his back.

He returned to the concierge's desk. 'Any news on the window?'

The concierge looked up. 'Good Evening, sir. How can I help you?'

'Good evening. Is there any news on getting my window unlocked?'

'It is in progress. My top priority sir.'

'Any idea how long?'

'Top of my list. Is there anything else I can help you with?'

The next morning Mark waited in the lobby and when the car arrived he got in. It was a different driver who spoke no English. 'Where are you taking me?' he shouted, and found himself dropped at offices deep in the city.

'I want to go to the site. Wait here.' He got out and the receptionist called someone who could translate, but when they returned outside the car had gone. At an office on the seventh floor a man was assigned to help him and with every question Mark asked the man disappeared to return with another stack of documents. When the pile was a foot high he stopped asking.

When a car finally arrived to take him to the worksite, they got stuck in traffic. After two hours of crawling through roads full of drivers on the brink of violence, he was delivered back to the apartment block.

Exhausted by the heat, he carried his pile of documents from the car.

At the front desk he waited for the concierge to look up.

'Sir? The window. Good news. We examined the window.'

'And?'

'There is no problem with the window.'

'It's not broken. I wanted to open it.'

'No, sir. Let me show you the air controls.'

As Mark collapsed on the sofa, he realised the tap was dripping again. He checked the tape. The tape had moved with the sofa.

When Arshad arrived, Mark greeted him like an old friend. Arshad smiled, dropped his tool bag and went into the bathroom. He bashed at the tap.

'Sir. All fixed.' The dripping had stopped.

'While you're here, could you look at the window?'

Arshad looked out over the landscape. 'Beautiful country,' he said and they both looked over the vista of half-constructed buildings, the clumps of workers bare-chested under their hi-visibility jackets and hard hats.

'Do you have a big family in Kerala, Arshad? Do you miss them?'

Arshad watched nervously as Mark unpeeled notes from the roll in his pocket. 'Can you unlock the window?'

Arshad went deep into his tool bag, and pulled out a handcrafted piece of metal, inserting it into the latch which sprang apart. He slid the window open.

A rush of air began, exchanging cold and warm, filtered and particulate, and the ceiling vents throbbed with this extra burden. The new air was hot and dirty with smoke and grit, but it felt good. Mark breathed it deep, and his stomach lurched at the drop to the ground below.

'Mother, sister, brother, sister, sister, auntie.'

'It must be hard, living here, away from them.'

Arshad screwed his face up, saving the question and its answer for later, his private time.

That night Mark moved the sofa so he could lie at the open window, and look up at the night sky, immersed in cool air.

The car arrived in the morning as Mark reached the lobby and drove him for a couple of miles before they became embedded in a traffic jam of luxury cars, ultra-loud horns blaring. After three hours, he exchanged some complicated signing with the driver, and found himself delivered back to the apartment block.

The furniture had moved again. The tape and his marker pen arrows on the marble had also moved. Both taps were now dripping.

The concierge came to his room. 'I am sorry you have needed to complain about our service. I will investigate with the member of staff involved.'

'I'm not complaining. I just think it maybe he could fix the tap once and for all, rather than having a daily visit.'

'I will check the record to find out who…'

'Arshad. Arshad Kamal. Talk to Arshad.'

'Sir.'

'He told me his name. He's from Kerala.'

'Sir, that is not possible. Our staff do not exchange personal information. Your complaint…'

'I'm not complaining. He fixes it, but the next day it's dripping again. I'm sure it's not his fault. And he helped me with the window.'

The concierge's face darkened as he examined the window, running his finger over the latch. 'I will get that fixed.'

Mark lay on the sofa that evening, watching the night sky with the double pinging of the taps of the two sinks dripping in and out of phase.

The next morning the driver took him to the construction site without a hitch. 'So where is everyone?' he asked.

The security man frowned. 'Holiday.'

The site manager offered him an interim inspection report to sign.

'I can't sign that…'

'Read. If anything is incorrectly described… you amend in the final report.'

'I haven't seen anything.'

'It's a good report. Thorough. Everything is covered.'

For seven hours he sat in a hut in baking heat, trying to review documents full of sentences with multiple sub-clauses and broken syntax, until his head pounded. The report was complete and consistent, but without connection to the world around him.

He signed the audit report, then went up the ladders to the tenth floor, and walked round the grit-covered steel of the concrete carcass and looked out over the expanse of turmoil and rubble below. The smoke still rose from the bonfire of cable reels and scrap material. He tore sheet after sheet from the report and let them fly through the unfenced open space of the building to scatter far below.

At his apartment the drip was fixed, but the window was locked again. The furniture had not moved. He lay on the sofa, squashing the remote control, flicking the television on. The programme was a compilation of animals dying in range of disasters: melting ice floes, drying lakes, newly formed deserts. He ran down the stairs to reception.

'Where is he? Arshad Kamal?'

The concierge smiled. 'No-one of that name works here.'

'He fixed my tap. Four days running.'

Mark pushed past him to the staff accommodation behind the reception desk.

'Sir, staff only.'

The room smelt ripe; sweat and feet and piss mixed with drains and rotting food. Rows of men lying on beds blinked at his intrusion and the sudden light. He peered into the darkness at the bunks.

'Arshad Kamal?'

The men began shouting angrily at him and began pushing him out, as if they did not want him to see the shame of their living conditions.

'English? Does anyone speak English?'

Still nothing. Nothing.

'I'm sorry,' he said to the concierge.

Outside he watched two men hose down and sweep the expanse of concrete around the apartment and when they had finished he lay on the steaming concrete, to stare upwards into the sun.

Someone had slipped a photograph under the door of his apartment. Arshad in a family photo, with a broad grin, and mother, sister, brother, sister, sister, auntie. When he slept, he dreamt of dark hunched figures pushing his furniture back to the correct places.

The next morning when the driver called Mark he was ready in the lobby. Everything was in place, for whatever he wanted to see. The car was outside, its engine ticking over.

The concierge eventually came over. 'Can I help sir? Your car is ready. Are you waiting for someone?'

'Yes. I'm waiting for Arshad Kamal.'

'Sir, I have not heard of this person.'

'Ok. I'll wait until he comes.' He settled into the sofa in the reception area.

A trace of controlled anger appeared on the concierge's face. 'This area… not for resident sitting. For visitors only.'

Mark flicked through the magazines on the table, with their adverts for expensive apartments in constructions nearby, and advertisement features on luxury restaurants. 'Gold dust was sprinkled on my rice for that extra magic…'

'Is it okay if I…?' He took the oud off the hook on the wall and examined it. The finish on this was rough and the fingerboard was warped. Not like the music shop oud. He strummed the strings anyway.

'Sir, for decoration. Not playing.'

'How do you tune it? Is it in fifths?'

The concierge did not answer, but Mark tuned it in fifths by ear, then slid his left hand up the fingerboard as he plucked the strings in a fast tremolo, using a snapped credit card as a plectrum. He began to sing tunelessly as he strummed.

Arshad Kamal. Arshad Kamal.

The concierge slammed the book closed on his desk and stood in front of Mark.

'You see, it's very important I see him. I promised I would send his family money if anything happened to him. Do you have the family address in Kerala?'

'Sir, your car is waiting.'

The driver was fiddling on his phone, the engine racing as the thermostat for the chiller kicked in, then eased off. Petrol was cheap in paradise. Petrol and people.

The concierge flicked a switch turning off the air conditioning in the lobby.

Within a few minutes beads of sweat appeared on the concierge's face and dripped from his nose onto the register he fastidiously updated. Mark could smell a rank odour developing in his own armpits. He strummed the oud violently, and sang.

> *Did you hear the story of*
> *Arshad Kamal?*
> *Used to work here,*
> *Had a terrible fall…*

One of the strings pinged broken.

'Do you have a spare? One string down. It will affect my playing.'

The concierge moved into his back office and Mark heard the whirr of his fan. He rushed into the reception toilet. On his return a brass tray with water, a jug of coffee, and pastries, heavy with nuts and sugar syrup, sat on the table.

He ate until his body was fired up by sugar and drank the coffee, and the water. He lifted the plate to lick off the last fragments and underneath found a replacement string for the oud.

He strummed five stings once more.

Did you hear the story of...
Arshad Kamal?

He spent the rest of the day playing the oud until the noise even annoyed him. That night he slept on the reception bench dreaming of a giant television on which every channel featured a falling man turning endlessly on a journey towards the ground. And the man was still screaming and falling after he'd turned the dream television off.

In the morning his own smell was overpowering. The glances as residents rushed through the lobby told him that the whole reception area was filling with the odour of his unwashed sweaty body.

'How many more days do you reckon?' he said to the petrified tree, the other resident of the reception area. Its desiccated leaves barely rustled up an answer.

A new tray appeared on the table, bearing a sandal, its red straps strained by an oversized foot, a Boston Red Sox cap, lined with grime and an iPod with a smashed screen and single earphone. He put them in his pocket. He would return them to Arshad.

'I think the oud might be tuned augmented fourths rather than fifths,' Mark said so the concierge could hear. He retuned it. Tritones were harder; you had to use harmonics and the strings were too old to ring properly.

The tray also held fruit, yoghurt, coffee and a guide to playing the oud in Urdu with diagrams showing correct positions (tick) and incorrect positions (cross).

'Good morning.' Mark waved to the concierge.

The concierge came over and began a little speech. 'We have an impossible situation. There have been complaints...'

'I have a complaint too...'

'From the other residents. Occupation of the reception area is not permitted. I have passed your request to the management for further investigation.'

'That's good. Very good.'

'So you will return to your room?'

'Yes.'

The concierge smiled, relieved, and put the oud back on the wall.

'When I have the results of the investigation. A truthful investigation.'

The concierge looked less happy.

'The investigation into the disappearance of Arshad Kamal. I need to get to the truth. His family are depending on me. I have spent a lot of time thinking about truth. There is the world documented in reports... and there is the world of facts. How do we connect the two?'

The concierge nodded. 'I have explained the facts very clearly...'

'Maybe they can't be connected, like dimensions, impossible concepts, imaginary numbers. All we can have is a story. Give me a good story that makes sense. I will return to my apartment and never open the window again.'

A steely rage appeared on the concierge's face. The battle was serious and Mark knew he was really stinking badly. The concierge went back to his office.

In the afternoon the concierge delivered two envelopes to Mark on a brass tray with an elaborate geometric design. One was from his employer, terminating his contract. The other was from the apartment management, ending his residency without notice. The concierge watched for his reaction, and departed with a slight bow.

Later a package appeared on the table, containing a boiler suit such as a building maintainer might wear. Mark put it on and discarded his filthy clothes. It felt good to have fresh clothes. In the toilet he splashed water over his face, armpits and groin.

When he emerged, his old clothes had gone along with his wallet and keys. In his boiler suit pocket he found a picture of a smiling girl in a sari. Her smile was so broad and generous that Mark felt moisture developing at a point deep in his eyes, so that it never emerged as tears. Arshad's girlfriend. Wife maybe. He wished they had put a name and address on it. A name at least. So he could repeat it to himself as he dozed.

In his sleep that night, his closed eyes reported to him the approach of a vehicle, endlessly pulling up and its occupants, men in uniforms, getting out and rushing towards him, always rushing.

In the morning when he woke, a tray had been set in front of him with the finest breakfast he could possibly imagine and next to it, a bundle of neatly folded fresh clothes. On top of the clothes was a pack of oud strings, each string tied in a loop by coarse silk in a different colour. And in a cloth bag, a tongue scraper and toothbrush with a tube of Ayurvedic toothpowder.

When he had changed the strings on the oud and they had stretched enough for the tuning to stabilise he sang his song again, and even though he kept forgetting the words, he heard the beating of pans in the kitchen, following its rhythm.

As he changed his clothes he realised he had now adopted Arshad's smell; a hint of methi seed, neem leaves, betel nut. It was a smell deep in his skin.

Every time he closed his eyes the television in his head played, showing an endless sweep of half-constructed buildings, always finishing in his apartment, where the furniture was moving, so slowly as to be barely perceptible.

Mark decided the oud should be tuned in diminished fourths. He broke a string as he retuned it. He knew the string would be replaced. He could break endless strings. There would come a point of revelation, after a hundred strings… a thousand strings broke… as he wound them tighter and tighter, and played until they snapped… then he would understand.

The concierge came over to see him, bowing slightly as he handed Mark a folded sheet of paper without an envelope or a tray. He did not have to open it to know that it explained in stark sentences how life was supported by strings held in tension and if one string broke the whole structure collapsed.

'I need to arrange my departure,' Mark said and played a sustained tremolo on a single note. The secret of a good tremolo was to lose all control, all sense of everything other than the continuous note, to become that note.

Here's the story of Arshad Kamal.

In the distance Mark heard another sound in harmony with him, a tapping, a beating of a drum, in the same insistent rhythm. An Indian flute. Finger cymbals. He breathed hot, dirty air and felt the approach of a marching band in the dazzle of sunlight.

The concierge was making a sequence of silent phone calls, watching as the van pulled up outside. A van to take him to the airport. It was so easy.

In the half-light of the van, Mark felt the need to whisper. 'You know,' he said to the man next to him, 'this really is paradise. Arshad Kamal explained it all to me…'

The Walk of Blood

M. A. HODGSON

He lived alone in the village, which is how rumours get started. 'He's an odd-looking bugger,' one mother said at the school gate. Everyone agreed, but when pressed, couldn't quite say why, although another woman who was known to have studied early 20th-century art had a theory about a face taken apart and put back together. Others joked about ugly sticks and being last in line.

They did not feel it necessary to elaborate on the link between the man's odd looks and internal demeanour. This connection had been cemented since people began telling stories. The odd-looking buggers were not the heroes and princes; they were the 'ones to watch out for'.

Children were warned, just in case.

'What's his name, anyway?'

No one knew for sure but there was a suggestion that it was a foreign-sounding surname, one that drew consonants together in a way that saw them rattle when spoken.

As for where he was from before he settled in the bungalow with the contents of a surprisingly large removal van, including more boxes labelled 'books' than any normal person would read in a lifetime, the feeling was that it must be Europe.

'One of them places we won't have to take all t'odds and sods from after Brexit.'

Apparently, he had once sent a parcel to a solicitor in London.

He didn't own any pets.

The fact that he did not respond when children limped behind him, imitating his gait, was considered another oddity, even after the discovery that he was profoundly deaf.

One thing that could not be disputed was that he was very old. Liver spots bruised his face and arms; lines carved memories across his face. His lips caved in towards a toothless mouth. The floss of his white hair barely covered his skull. But beneath the wiry curl of his eyebrows, his round bright eyes remained vigilant.

Despite his age and infirmity, he liked to take a walk every morning. He kept to the same route, turning left out of his stone cottage and entering the woods bordered by cornfields.

No one could remember when the Walk of Blood was first mentioned. It began as a rumour, which, just as it began to die down, was revived as an uneasy joke.

It was thought to have come from something overheard, as despite being deaf, or perhaps because of it, the man liked to talk to himself.

On the day he was followed, the man left his cottage at the usual time. It was mid-July; the paving slabs were severe with heat and even the best-tended gardens sagged and slumped.

Supported by his stick, he made his way into the woods. He didn't hear the shuffling whispers of the three boys who followed him, just kids of maybe 12 or 13, but he sensed their presence. He didn't protest. Let them follow. There was nothing anybody could do to him now.

The ghosts of all the dogs he'd owned walked beside him. He would have liked a new companion, but had not expected to live this long after the last one left.

He sometimes forgot his age. He had lied about it when he joined the resistance and it was easier to continue to do so. He had been tall for his age and broad shouldered back then, before his body began to shrink and fold in on itself. In the boldness of youth, he had stood alongside others in protest on the streets of Warsaw, but many had fallen at his side and he had gone underground.

There were others who had fallen, too. He had left them behind in the cities of occupied France and later on the Normandy beaches.

The children who followed him today, they knew nothing of this life. Their parents, too. He could give them all a history lesson. How his fellow Poles and the Czechs and the North Africans and the Indians and the rest fought alongside the Allies. But people didn't want lessons. They didn't want to be reminded.

He had never thought of himself as a hero, but he had been quietly proud of his contribution during the war. This meant nothing now. He knew what people thought of him; some of them at least. They had told him. He was a scrounger, taking money from the state, stealing from British pensioners. It didn't matter that he had made this country his home, worked hard all his life, paid taxes.

He had been on the bus heading into town when it happened, a couple of years earlier, not long after the Brexit vote. A group of men got on, smartly dressed in polo shirts and jeans, black zip-up jackets. They invited attention from the start, shouting slogans, staring down any passengers who glanced at them. It seemed they were heading to some kind of protest march; one of them had an England flag round his shoulders with the slogan: 'Refugees not welcome'.

He supposed he counted as a refugee. Driven from his homeland. But he had chosen not to go back, and to make a life here instead, alongside those he had fought for.

At the next stop, the young woman sitting next to him got off and one of the men took the seat. He was a handsome young lad; blue eyes framed by long dark lashes, high cheekbones, wide mouth. His hair was shaved close to his head and covered by a tweed cap.

'All right, grandad.'

He nodded politely and kept his head down but this wasn't enough.

'Where are you heading, then?'

'Into town, shopping.'

As soon as the words left his lips, their jagged trace of an accent condemned him.

They pulled him from his seat, ignoring his protests.

The other passengers watched it happen. They looked shocked, but did nothing.

He followed the path through the woods, trying to ignore the ache in his leg. The whole world had been at war and he had somehow survived, only to be thrown from the step of a bus.

The three young lads were now following him in plain sight.

They had fallen quiet, perhaps nervous, perhaps bored. Children seemed to have such a short attention span nowadays.

At the end of the line of trees, there was an opening to the cornfields. Instead of looping round for his usual return walk, he stepped through the gap.

The field stretched out before him. The seeds he had spread from his pockets in the spring had buried into the rich earth. It was a long way from where the bodies were buried but it would have to do. Roots and shoots had burst forth. And at the heart of each plant, a bold red flower.

He stood for a moment, observing the field of corn, dotted with hundreds of poppies. He stepped out on to the field of tiny wounds and began his Walk of Blood. This was his remembrance. His silent protest.

The Unplayable

BRUCE HARRIS

I saw him on Wednesday, August 15th 1990, by the frozen food counter in Sainsbury's, picking things up, peering at them, and putting them back. A woman in the next aisle was gazing at him with an odd mixture of maternity and lust.

The nineteen-year-old Lex Winter, reserve team professional footballer, was as gorgeous a youth as I'd ever seen. Almost exactly six feet tall, naturally dark-skinned, with jet black short hair and disconcerting blue green eyes, he had a perfect torso fully emphasised by a thin light blue top, bare untattooed arms, and leg-hugging jogging bottoms. Never mind a punter, I thought; I'd do him for free.

Yes, at the time, I was rent. Ian Sims, twenty-one years old, failed student and failed genius of cuisine. Once the lack of academic brain had been established, it was sweating in some tyrant's kitchen for sod all or the game. The game, for the moment, won.

False modesty to hell, I was as cute as a basket of kittens, big brown hazel eyes, flashing white teeth, blondish hair I'd spend hours on, and a few other decidedly non-kittenish accoutrements as useful professional equipment. I'd lost contact with all the family except my aunt, Roz Forbes, drama lecturer, and my dad's younger sister, who called herself the black cow of the family, bohemian, chain-smoking, foul mouthed. The last time I'd visited her in her city flat, a kind of Bedouin tent with a roof on, she looked at me and said, 'Ian, darling, I do believe you're on the fucking game.' I wondered how she knew and begged for her silence. She looked me up and down.

'I don't shop people, sweetheart, even to my dear brother. Or should that be especially? But be careful, my lovely. Be bloody careful.'

Lex's eyes flicked at me and stayed just too long.

'Too much choice?' I said, and I got the eyes full on. I had to catch my breath.

'What are you supposed to do with this stuff?' he said, as if we were already mates.

We fumbled on for a few minutes, something about the landlady of his so-called 'digs' being away on holiday and him now 'pissed off with pizza and Chinese', but it was all irrelevant flannel and we both knew it. We were in my place, a shag nest by the river, in thirty minutes and naked in forty. By then, I was pretty good at finding out soon enough what really floated a guy's boat, and often it had to be a matter of finding out. Some didn't have the words, some didn't have the nerve, and some didn't know, believe it or not. There had to be protection if needed – Aids was still at the top level of consciousness in 1990. Otherwise, whatever. The graphic details of this session with Lex would take too long to go into; it seemed, for him, to be like a dam bursting, both mentally and physically. The main surprise about it, from my point of view, was that he was mainly submissive; I say mainly for the sake of accuracy, because there are few entirely one way or the other, whatever the stereotypes, and believe me, I should know. How much that squares with the image of macho footballers, I don't know, but I could see the conflict in him between what turned him on and what he thought should. I worked carefully on him with the benefits of long experience, and his beautiful, athletic body reacted to me like a man in a desert taking a drink.

After some expenditure of time and energy, we lay together for a few minutes. He knew normal gay etiquette made it my turn and I had to remind myself that this one was pleasure, not duty; not every punter worries too much about my turn. He surprised me with his expertise and obvious enjoyment of teasing me, carefully, expertly, back and front; he teased and teased, taking me to the edge and back again, until I was gasping and begging to be allowed to come, and when I did, I closed my eyes and went wherever that place is longer and higher than I could remember having done for weeks.

So we lay together again, this time with that strange post-coital thing of two naked men realising they actually know next to nothing about each other.

'What do you do?' I said, for the sake of saying something, like the Queen.

'I'm a pro footballer.'

'Oh.' I nodded slowly. I'd had everything, up to and including astronauts. Why they feel they need to impress their whore, I never could understand. But they do.

'No, I am. Reserve team at the moment. Contract until twenty-one. Good money, but harder work than most people think.'

'I suppose.' Then I made a mistake. He'd just mentioned working for a living, reminding me that I did too, so I flicked on my answer phone to get the messages.

'Hi – saw your ad and picture. Like it. I'm in town on Wednesday p.m.; how about something. I usually top; maybe a little CP with afters. Nothing heavy. Talk to you soon.'

'Hello. I don't know how happy you are topping middle-aged guys – real sub stuff, for me. Make me obey; anything, I mean anything – '

An odd choking shout sounded on my right; Lex was standing up, looking down on me, his eyes blazing. I flicked the machine off.

'Rent. God, you're fucking rent. This is a set-up, right? Pay up or the papers? Bastard – I thought you were just a guy – '

By this time, I'd got to my feet too and was trying to put my arms round him.

'No, fuck off,' he said unconvincingly, pushing distractedly against me. 'How much do you want? I've got cash – '

'Lex, no – '

The split personality, aggression and submission, wildness and gentleness, which soon became familiar, then showed itself in all its spectacular opposition. He squared up, and suddenly I could see the muscles in the shoulders and arms, the total absence of spare flesh, more vividly than ever. He punched me on the cheek, only just missing my eye, and I saw red myself. No punter, I'd decided long ago, was ever going to knock me about like that. I punched him back, hitting almost exactly the same spot. For a minute or two, we both massaged the wound, both of us, I think, surprised at the force and pain of the blows. Then we looked at each other and dissolved into giggles like two little kids. We weren't much more, when all's said and done. I grabbed the moment.

'I didn't do you as a punter, Lex. I did you because I fancied you like hell. And I was right.'

From then on, it seemed that we were made. I'd become a cynical bastard, as indifferent to punters as most of them were to me, but he'd pressed a button which I hadn't realised was still there. I even got onto boring old football, just to sound interested.

'I want to get to be something like ———— ', he said, mentioning the name of a famous footballer, I assumed, though it meant nothing to me.

'The boss says that guy is unplayable.' Now there was real enthusiasm in his voice; the whole spasm of temper had faded, like a kid after a tantrum.

'Unplayable?'

'You know. Impossible to stop. He scores goals for fun. That's what I want to be. Unplayable.'

We continued to see each other off and on, precariously, Lex terrified that the media would somehow detect his regular visits; reserve team player or not, the death of Justin Fashanu in 1988 meant the subject of gay footballers was still high on the media agenda and Lex was paranoid about being followed or 'shopped'. It didn't seem to occur to him that the most obvious person to shop him would be me, and his instinctive, if mysterious, trust in me restored something of my severely battered self-belief. He didn't like the way I earned a living – understandably enough, I suppose. When I asked him what he would suggest, he would have one of his long, distracted sulks, like a kid whose game has been pinched.

'If I make the big time, the twenty grand a week stuff, that'll be that, Ian.'

Two or three months in, he started getting games in the full team rather than the reserves, and bringing me press cuttings about his matches; seeing me, he said, had improved his game. At first, the logic of this mystified me. But I think, with me, the guilt and recrimination had gone; he could allow his guilty submissive side to be satisfied. Guys whose lives often need them to be aggressive and assertive, which is most of them, can lose off the gentler side, the desire to give and be enjoyed by someone; it becomes associated with guilt and fear, especially the fear of vulnerability, in a world where many people are more likely to find male vulnerability exploitable and contemptible than engaging. Lex came to me, had his fill, and went back out to play the game he needed to play, in more ways than one.

I began to ache for him when he wasn't there, and to resent the guys I had to deal with. Lex was incredibly athletic, fastidiously clean and fantastic looking; everyone else paled beside him. He told me sometimes about needing to tell stories about women to keep the guys happy.

'You should hear the way they talk about women,' he would say. 'In the dressing room, talking about their lays as if they're waving their cocks at each other. "I gave it one straight off. Hungry, man." "It was a woof-woof, right enough, but it blew a beautiful job." It. I fucked it. The It. The Thing. But if any guy dares to talk about making them the 'its', they're, like, "oh, gross, man, gay is so gross."'

Then everything changed very rapidly, as it sometimes does. He arrived in a state of real excitement, his face lit up. He was going to be transferred, he said, into another club in the same division, except the manager had more or less guaranteed him first team football. And a lot more money.

'Come with me, Ian. You and me. Get out of this. I need you with me; I can't do it without you. Come with me.'

I hesitated, and he was hurt. He thought I wasn't convinced about the money and showed me the contract. Eye-stretching as the pay was, I still needed time to think, provoking another protracted sulk, which we got out of with a bathroom session – bathrooms had enormous potential, and Lex liked variety.

While he lay in my arms afterwards, I told him how difficult it had been to make myself free and independent, how he was the only person in the world I would even think about giving that up for, but I had to have a little time and space. I needed, for once, to talk to someone older, so I phoned Roz. She listened without interrupting, as she always has.

'I'm 95 per cent sure I should go for it, Roz. What do you think?'

A kind of snort sounded down the line.

'Heavens, sweetheart, I'm no reed to lean on. My relationship history is like a battlefield after the battle, and all the corpses are me. Your dad could tell you if you asked him; in fact, he'd probably tell you even if you didn't ask him.'

'He might if he was talking to me.'

A heavy silence. 'Oh, Ian, darling.'

A vivid image came to my mind of my father staring up at me from his favourite armchair, his thin face pale and his eyes narrowed in the certainty of his utter contempt. Even now, those last few days could force tears. I tried to speak, but Roz got there first.

'Listen, Ian, you've always been a strong, determined little bugger, and if this guy isn't for you, someone will be. Get off the game, darling, because that will only ever last for a while before it starts to destroy you. How do I know, never mind how I know. Give Lex a go, sweetheart. Sometimes the chance is worth taking. I've had a few fuck up on me, yes, but while they lasted, I was having a ball.'

Roz clinched it. Lex and I put down a deposit on a flat about thirty miles from his club. He told them he was in a flat share and that's all he wanted for the moment. He was twenty years old; no-one thought much about it. We found a greater bliss and peace in that place than either of us had thought possible. It was a good deal bigger than my little shag nest, and I appointed myself in charge of décor and equipping the place. In the very centre of town, where people drifted in and out in their thousands and no-one noticed who came and who went, we lived our dream. Even the downside – Lex was an untidy sod, unused to regular meal times and not good at planning the next day, and I dare say I had my own set ways after being essentially alone for so long – was fascinating, revelatory, liberating.

By late 1992, we were a couple in every sense of the term that mattered, though even then, problems remained. Other members of the team had women who came to watch them and went to club dos with them, and Lex's youth and inexperience were wearing thin to explain his lack of a partner. He kept on with the line that he hit the town well away from the club so as not to get into the papers.

We had to have some kind of social life, and for that we relied almost entirely on my friends, some of whom remained on the game. Sex workers develop a kind of ethic of their own when it comes to the punters; even if you think you might get paid for going to the media with a 'name', you know well enough that your business will be ruined for ever afterwards, because no one will trust you any more. Names are also likely to have squads of lawyers behind them. Discretion is practical politics as well as professional etiquette, and I wasn't too concerned about them shopping Lex. In any case, none of them could prove anything.

In mid-November 1992, we met up with Rick Pierce and his new lover Mark Southern. Rick had that elastic, high jumper's build which some guys are crazy about. He'd dipped in and out of prostitution after running from an oppressive Northern household; for a good while, he pretended the 'I only do it for money and I'm not really gay' line. Those guys do exist, yes, but he wasn't really one of them; a punter we had in common once described him to me as a 'really thirsty boy; I swear he'd do it for the hell of it'. Mark worked in a hotel restaurant, the same hotel which Rick occasionally used for picking up. Mark was quiet and dark; he smiled incessantly, if enigmatically. Their flat was very similar to ours, with a balcony and a view; we all felt at home. Both being 'foodies', Mark and I got on well enough, though something about him disturbed me, perhaps the way those little dark eyes darted about and wouldn't meet mine. He and Rick had first got it together in the hotel gents, risking Mark getting the sack; Rick described him to me as a 'sweet, uncomplicated guy who walks the wild side now and then; enough said'.

Late at night, after a drink or two, Rick looked at Lex and smiled.

'Now, tell me to butt out, Lex, but I only ever look at the sports back pages when a sexy picture catches my eye. The other day, that's what happened, and the guy with the oiled thighs on show didn't just look like you, he had the same name. How's that happen, Lex?'

We looked at each other, reaching a mutual decision; sooner or later, we thought, this had to happen, and it might as well be now with guys who were friends enough to trust. Lex had had a drink, and I thought his pleasure at relaxing his secret was mostly about that, until, only a week later, he phoned me in the mid-afternoon.

'Ian, I'm coming home with Brent Morrison.'

'Oh, God. What – to eat?'

Brent Morrison was a name I knew well enough by then, the captain of Lex's team, a guy in his mid-thirties playing out a solid career before heading into management. I knew he was married, with three young kids. He'd been magic with Lex from the first, advising him, encouraging him, showing him around. Lex knew he helped the new young players as part of his job; he balanced the taciturn Welsh manager in the familiar hard man, soft man combination, but he appreciated Brent all the same.

'He asked if he could visit where I lived; I couldn't think how to put him off. Maybe, after Rick and Mark, we could start – you know – taking it on?'

So Brent came to dinner, and said nice things about our place and my food. Lex and I looked at each other in the kitchen, question marks on both our faces, wondering whether the guy had worked it out. He was a big man, calm-eyed and curiously graceful on his feet, relaxed with himself and others.

A big, verbal coming out proved to be unnecessary. Lex and I were very easy with each other by then; we touched a lot, kissed each other casually, exchanged looks to check on how the other felt. In our own place, it would have taken a guy a lot less sensitive to people than Brent Morrison not to work out what we were all about.

The crucial moment happened quite incidentally. I put Lex's coffee down in front of him; he was finicky about his coffee, having it just the way he liked it. He sipped it and smiled, putting his hand on the back of my neck and pulling my face down to kiss. We had, just for a second, forgotten Brent was there. We both realised simultaneously, and his eyebrows went up as two anxious faces turned suddenly in his direction.

'Don't worry,' he said, 'it's under my hat for now. It comes out – you come out – when you judge the moment and the ground's been prepared a bit. I knew Justin Fashanu; I liked him. That's not going to happen to anyone in my team.'

Lex and I were both blown away with the idea that at last, we had a friend inside football. I even listened to them both explaining more about the game, to have a better idea of what Lex actually did day by day.

So the hammer in my guts was all the greater when, less than a week later, in my nearest store, Lex's name was plastered all over the local paper.

'Town's Young Pro Living with Rent Boy', it said, in big black letters. Seven words, and I had to read them again and again, eyes flickering across the page to try and make myself believe it was really happening. 'A family friend –' Family friend? Who the hell? '–describes the relationship as having lasted for some time. "Lex Winter has always been gay, as far as I know," he said, "he hasn't come out because football won't let him come out."' Well, right enough for that, I thought. But the identity of the family friend tormented me; I wondered wildly if it could be Roz Forbes.

I dashed back to the flat and Lex was already there, sitting on the sofa, pale and bewildered. It was only just after ten in the morning. He'd seen the paper in the garage when he got his petrol and turned right back, thinking that the ground would already be swarming with reporters – as it was.

'I can't believe it,' he said, in the half-strangled voice that normally precedes the long sulk. 'Brent Morrison. I trusted the bastard, I really did. The skip. Of all people.'

I was just about to agree with him, with an enormous sense of relief that my aunt was off the hook, when I made myself reflect that, if I could jump to such rapid and devastating conclusions, perhaps he was too.

'We don't know, Lex. "Family friend" is hardly him, is it?'

The first knock on the door coincided almost exactly with the first ring of the phone, both of them immediately crushing any notions we might have that the media would still be working out exactly where we lived. Someone had told them that as well.

'Lex?' someone shouted from behind the door, and the use of his first name by a disembodied, unknown voice had a sinister edge to it. 'If Lex Winter is in there, we're offering the chance for you to put your side of the story. Don't let them have it all their way, Lex. Come out and talk to us.'

'Stay quiet,' I whispered to him. 'Stay very quiet.'

For a minute or so, he did, then he lost his head, for some reason, and stamped out on to the balcony to see if anyone of them were outside. The shouts, along with the whirl and clatter of cameras, started as soon as he stepped out. I saw his frame silhouetted against the increasing brightness of the morning, his back held awkwardly, frozen as if arrested by a beam of light.

I dragged him back in; we retreated to the bedroom, making sure every door that could be was locked. For over an hour, we lay beside each other on the bed, frozen, ignoring the knocks, shouts and phone buzzes. Then a different tone sounded, and I saw it was my mobile. I let it take a message, and picked it up afterwards. It was Rick, speaking as if someone had shut him in a cell.

'Ian, it was Mark. He's devastated. Late night at the club, blabbering to some guy he'd just met who turned out to be from the Sentinel. He's quiet as a mouse a lot of the time, but when he takes what he takes and puts booze on top of it – Ian, mate, I'm so sorry. Come to us. At least pick up on me, Ian, for fuck's sake…'

At that moment, I couldn't have talked to him – I couldn't have talked to anyone. I remember it registering that the press men can't have had the number of my mobile, because Rick's was the only call I'd had in the last two hours. How long it would have been before we'd taken action of some kind, I don't know, but we noticed the noise outside the flat door dying down rapidly, and then a different kind of knock sounded, more muted, less in your face.

'Lex and Ian? It's Brent, Brent Morrison. I think I can help.'

We let him in and locked the door behind him.

'OK,' he said, settling himself into an armchair. Apart from a slightly faster pace of talking, he didn't seem disturbed at all.

'The manager of the apartment block is out there with a couple of policemen. Residents have been screaming blue murder. They will at least make that lot retreat out of the building, so we've got a little breathing space.'

He appeared to be considering something for a moment; he was the kind of man who always tended to think before he spoke.

'Firstly, I'll tell you what the club wants you to do. The club wants me to take Lex back with me – just Lex – for a press conference early this afternoon, where we're going to say Ian's your flat mate, you've only known him for a few weeks, you didn't know what he was up to, their source was a young gay on the make – we'll imply blackmail – and then the club's lawyers will look at legal action if the papers persist.'

He looked up and saw the expressions on our faces. We were both momentarily struck dumb.

'Now,' and he looked straight into our faces, 'I'll tell you what I think you should do. You both have cars parked in that underground car park that serves the building?'

We nodded.

'They might know what Lex drives, but they certainly won't know what you drive, Ian. Go down in the lift while you have the chance, leave in Ian's car with Lex's head down on the back seat, go to some relative or friend they can't possibly know – can you think of anyone?'

Lex still looked bewildered, shell-shocked almost, but I leaned forward and nodded vigorously; yes, I certainly could think of someone.

'Then take a few days to think it through. It should be what you want to do, not what people can bounce you into. You need time. We'll tell them you've gone to ground and we don't know where.'

We agreed so completely and readily with Brent's idea – we were both very young and very frightened - that we didn't stop to worry about whether the club would take it out on Brent, though he left soon after that to take up a managerial post, and I think he'd probably already fixed that up. Big thick footballers is just one more sporting cliché.

We fled to Roz's for a few days, and she, bless her, was delighted to have us.

'Thank God, if She really is up there. I was going out of my mind. I didn't dare phone in case they were tracking – they do that, you know? Now we'll take it easy and think it over, boys.'

Two days later, Brent Morrison phoned me on my mobile, a number which he'd clearly kept strictly to himself, and he gave us the club line, hastily agreed by manager, chairman and backers. The club would buy out Lex's contract in full, all four years of it, to prevent anything going to court; they were afraid we might sue for unfair dismissal, Brent said. The condition was that Lex and I needed to simply disappear out of their lives for ever.

That night, we mulled it over around Roz's huge antique mahogany dining table, after Roz and I had joined forces to produce a very special meal. 'Whatever has to be decided, we can at least do it on a pleasantly full stomach,' she said. Lex talked hesitantly, softly, the way he does when something is really on his mind.

Roz and I watched and listened, but she had hold of my hand under the table and she squeezed it from time to time.

'If we sell the flat as well, we'll be fine to set up somewhere else. Maybe Ian could start a restaurant, where he can be the boss, like he's always wanted. I just can't face it, guys; the abuse, the spitting, the faces, every time I take a corner, every time I go near the touchline. The dressing room mocking; the turned backs. There are gay pros; I know by their eyes, every changing room I've ever been in has at least one set of those eyes. Mine meet theirs; I know, he knows, and neither of us do anything about it. Yes, they'll be some on our side, but how many of them are going to be there, in the ground, when I have to go out and play?'

So the restaurant it was, and still is, twenty years on. I went into my business as the boss, which is the best way to do it. Lex had a ten-year, highly successful career as a model. When I first suggested the idea, he practically laughed himself into a fit, then I told him about the friends I had who'd said how incredible he'd be at it. He still resisted; he was adamant he wouldn't do nude stuff or porn, and I said he wouldn't have to. Lex, by then in his early twenties, with his dark looks and perfectly toned and proportioned body, was a clothes horse for the stuff many companies wanted to sell, and when he got more confidence with it, he did a few topless sessions for the gay papers. But the picture which almost every gay man – and quite a few women – had on their walls for a good while was the one he did for a certain underwear company. Iconic is a much over-used word, but iconic is what it was.

Lex in his early forties is a little bit beefier, but he can still kick a ball about and does charity matches occasionally. My father is no longer with us, but my mother and I have picked up the pieces and I see her from time to time.

Well over twenty-five years later, civil partnerships and same sex marriage have been made legal and discrimination against gay people has been made illegal. In almost every walk of life, including some very famous names indeed, gay people have felt able to come out to be and live as they are.

But since the suicide of persecuted Justin Fashanu in 1988, not a single solitary example yet exists of an out gay professional footballer. For the gay world, football, the most widely supported sport in the world, remains the unplayable, still locked in its own bigoted and anachronistic isolation.

Meet, me.

BEX O'GORMAN

As I lie reading the *Jackie* magazine, I imagine the girl in the picture kissing me. It feels tingly in my pants. I put my fingers down the front of my knickers and rub the moist skin. It feels nice. Really nice.

I begin to get lost in the imagined kiss when something alien touches my hand. I jump and open my eyes. As sit up I feel a sharp pain from between my legs, like the time I jarred my thumb. I stand and lift the skirt that mother insists that I wear, to see what looks like a lump. As I am looking the lump is getting smaller but I can feel it going into me like it's actually a part of me. I quickly pull down the knickers I have pulled the little ribbon bows off, but see nothing. There is a strange sensation and I can still feel it so I get out a mirror.

Being careful to lock the door in case my mother comes in, I pull the skirt that mother insists that I wear up to my waist. I sit on the floor and put the mirror between my legs. I realise how ridiculous it is that at the age of thirteen, I have never looked at what mother calls my 'privates'. Biology is not open for discussion at our house and I have never seen my parents – or anybody else for that matter – naked. At school, biology lessons are about plants and animals. Never bodies. I don't talk about what I have 'down there'. I don't really want to talk about my body; it's embarrassing and I don't feel the same about mine as Jess does about hers. All I know I have learned from Jess who talks constantly about what's in her pants and what's in 'Tommy the Stud's' pants. Jess says she'd have sex with 'Tommy the Stud' if he asked her. I hate 'Tommy the Stud'.

As I look at the peach and brown mass in the mirror, I know that I have no idea what I am looking for because I don't know what a normal vagina actually looks like. Jess never said anything about hers growing something out of it, and I know she'd have said. I always agree with her, like it's happening to me as well but it's only because I fancy her. I need to get to a library. I want to know what it is so when Jess tells me about hers, I'll sound like I already know and she might not see me as her naïve mate. She won't ever think about me like I do about her though.

Her unconscious naked body lay motionless on the prepared sheet, the instruments delicately placed beside her on the floor.

'Do you touch yourself, Laura?' Jess has a smile like cling film on leftovers.

'I do it all the time. It gets really wet and I rub it with my finger and it starts to feel really warm. Then I get a fluttery feeling and I can't touch it again for a while after that.'

She is looking at me and waiting for a response.

'Yeah, mine does that too.'

The reality is mine does far more than that, but I know I can't talk to her about it. I'm relieved when she spots her father's car.

'See ya tomorrow, babe,' she says as she hugs me and kisses me on the cheek.

I feel that now familiar tingle and my face feels as though it's on fire. I push her away and start to run.

'You alright, Laura?' she calls after me.

Without looking back, I tell her I'll see her tomorrow.

I reach for the scalpel and assess the blade. I am rushing. Replacing the blade to its position among the surgical equipment, I stop.

The books are spread in a semi-circle around me. With my legs apart, I am attempting to compare the labelled diagrams with what I am furiously manoeuvring before the mirror. Had my body been created on a Spirograph, I might see more of a resemblance to the sketches in the textbooks. The labels seem clear though and I have all of the bits listed. What it is not telling me is what is beyond

'Opening of Vagina'. There's something called the 'Hymen' but it doesn't look like the disappearing lump that I saw and it says nothing about it growing and shrinking. I decide to explore further.

There's something just inside the opening. Is that the hymen? On further reading, I realise it is not. I need the lump to come out again so I can see it, so I think about how it happened the first time.

I close my eyes and lie on my back in front of the mirror. Instead of thinking about the girl in the magazine, I think about Jess. She doesn't kiss me on the cheek this time but holds my face and kisses me fully on my mouth. She tells me that she fancies me too and kisses my neck. The tingling feeling starts and as I touch myself, I imagine Jess's hands touching my chest, but it's a flat chest – like a boy's. I begin to feel the lump stirring but do not want to open my eyes and spoil the fantasy that it is Jess touching me so I carry on. Just as she described, it starts to feel warm. Now that I know about the lump, I am aware that it is growing. I move my fingers and stroke what feels like a tube coming out of the 'Opening of Vagina' described in the book. I am surprised when this too feels good. I lift my head and open my eyes to see what looks like a well-used, flesh-coloured crayon, straight and moving when my fingers touch it. I stop and shuffle closer to the mirror. The crayon begins to retreat.

I look to my unsteady hands and clasp them together making the latex squeak. I take a long breath in through my nose.

As my mother sprays the starch onto my father's shirt collars, I am nervous as I say the words I have practised.

'I need to go to the doctors, Mum.'

'Why?'

'I think there's something wrong with me, down there.'

She holds the spray in position but doesn't expel the aerosol. Her face drains of colour but she doesn't look at me.

'Down where, Laura?'

'In my knickers. Something has been happening.'

She begins spraying the starch furiously and over working the shirts in a way that she has warned me against during what she calls 'life lessons'.

'We'll go and make it stop. I told them that you didn't need to keep it but they wouldn't take it away. I knew I was right. A mother always knows best.'

I am not sure at first what she is talking about but it begins to dawn on me that she knows exactly what's wrong with me.

'Take what away, mum? What do you mean?'

She picks up the bundle of hanging shirts and leaves the room, closing the door behind her. This is my mother's code for 'do not follow me'. What hasn't she told me about, well, me?

The deep breath feels like water rushing to my lungs. I realise that I am only waiting for the inevitable drowning and I am irked at my own time wasting.

Since that day, there have been no further discussions about it. We have spent the last couple of years resetting the understanding that this is my elephant and no matter how much it fills the room, we live edging around it and not giving it a name.

I retrieve the clothes that I bought with my sixteenth birthday money from behind the wardrobe. The underpants feel different to my usual knickers. I slide the jeans up my legs and fasten the buttons at the opposite side to the skirts I have always worn. The shirt feels stiff and the arms are too long. Nothing fits properly because I couldn't try anything on before getting it home. Even here I have to be careful.

Mother took the lock from my bedroom door not long after my fifteenth birthday when I asked her to call me Jude. I understood more about my condition by then. I had asked the doctor how common hermaphroditism was and was told:

'Figures are obscure.'

The word stuck with me, hence my chosen name.

Mother freaked. Now, at sixteen, I should be allowed some privacy, but she insists that these 'ridiculous notions' cannot be allowed to develop.

She will start to regain consciousness in the next four minutes and, confident in my own ability during the dry runs, I know I haven't factored in a moving body.

I take the scissors and hack at my hair until there is barely anything left. I head to the bathroom and lather up what is left with my father's shaving foam.

As I am shaving the last remnants of Laura away, I hear my mother calling for the daughter that she desperately wants me to be. Nervous because she is climbing the stairs, I rush to finish and nick the skin on my head.

She opens the bathroom door and I drop the razor. Her mouth twists as she takes on-board the sight before her. The momentous meeting of Jude and my mother. Her voice cracks.

'I don't deserve this Laura. Why are you hurting me like this? I have only ever given you love. I have given you everything that a girl could possibly want or need.'

I tell her that I am not a girl; I am Jude. She walks toward me and slaps my face. It is my reminder that my existence is not about me, but her. I am not her child, I'm her possession and my purpose is to ensure all I do is about her being my mother rather than me being a person in my own right.

'Get those clothes off and cover your head, Laura.' She leaves the room. I have to get away from here. From her.

Whilst her heart rate is down, the blood flow will remain manageable.

I got my first taste of freedom from mother whilst in student digs, and since I had spent this precious time eliminating Laura, and there being no question of Jude returning home after graduation, I found a flat near the Uni. The flat is Jude's domain. Despite having lived here for the best part of fifteen years, mother has never been. When she wants to see Laura, she phones, always careful to open the conversation with '*It's mum*' so that Laura knows to speak. Then she has to put on those clothes and the 'real hair', go and be ushered into their house to be told how pretty she is and asked about any men in her life. Only once Laura mentioned me.

At the flat, I am checking the views on my profile and seeing if there are any messages.

Hi. My name is Ruth. I am 36, divorced and have two great kids. Blah blah blah.

Delete.

I'm Karen. I love partying and having a great time. Blah blah blah.
Delete.

Hello Jude. My name is Jenny. I have looked at your profile a few times and have plucked up the courage to contact you. If you fancy a drink sometime, send me a reply. Everything you might want to know about me is on my profile. J x

I go to her profile so I can see her picture more clearly and find out a bit about her. As I click it open, a larger, clearer picture surprises me. She is pretty. There is something familiar about her. I read the page.

Name: Jenny Aster.

Age: 33.

Occupation: Veterinary assistant.

I continue to read through the profile and decide to email her, leaving her my number.

I glance towards the ketamine bottle and decide to refill the syringe.

I strap my breasts down for the date. They have remained in a pubescent state so this isn't a massive job. I select a shirt and trousers, then add my waistcoat. Aftershave on, hair parted, shoes on, wallet and keys in my pocket, I head to the restaurant.

When I walk in, she is already there. She stands to greet me as I approach the table. As she smiles, I realise why she looks familiar; her eyes and smile remind me of my mother. I am instantly revolted but do not show it, masking it as I have on many occasions with the woman herself. When I awkwardly kiss her cheek, I notice that her perfume is not the same as mother's and decide that I won't make my excuses just yet.

Conversation is flowing and I find myself laughing easily and enjoying Jenny's company. We discuss work and I talk about accountancy. I mention my early aspirations of becoming a mechanic and my mother's refusal to hear of it. She picks up one of my soft hands. Inspecting it and smiling, she tells me that she's glad because she doesn't like rough hands. My stomach churns.

'I think you and mother would get along famously.'

After doing so, I pull her breast across her chest and check the tautness of the skin. I pick up the marker and begin to draw the dashed lines that my blade will soon follow.

Things are going well with Jenny. There have been times during the couple of dates when I have felt genuinely at ease with her. I feel bad for keeping my condition from her. She is really open about herself. I know where she lives, works, who her friends are, how often they see one another. I know about her happy, normal childhood and where she grew up. I know that her boss leaves an array of animal medication in his unlocked car in case he is called out of hours. She knows nothing about the real me.

As I finish the last line, I know that my last chance to allow her to remain a complete woman has passed and I find the scalpel between my fingers again.

During our fourth date, Jenny asks if I would like to go back to her house after the performance. I have been expecting the question since the second date due to the hints she has been dropping. I have managed to avoid it so far with clichés such as 'I don't want to rush things,' but it seems my platitude well has run dry. She looks at me as though I am the wine she has looked forward to all week, then turns her head back towards the stage, revealing her profile and I almost double-take. Her make-up is different. She is wearing colours which compliment her outfit. The eye shadow is almost exactly the shade mother wears. When I do not give her an answer, she looks back to me and the hue of her eyelid makes me feel queasy. Panic registers on her face and I know that I must either walk away or commit to the next move.

The polished blade glints in the stark bathroom lighting.

I am putting my things in the overnight bag, checking each item against the list. The plan is to meet at Jenny's house and have lunch before we head to the hotel and spend our first night together.

I have driven past her house so know the area quite well. We have decided to take her car so I phone a taxi which drops me in the next street. She is preparing lunch so I enter through the open back door into the kitchen. She smiles *that* smile as I walk in and offers me a drink. She asks if I want to put my bag straight into the car but it has my phone in it and I tell her I want to let mother know when we are about to leave.

I ask to use the bathroom and she explains where it is.

'I'll put my bag by the front door on the way.'

As I reach the door, I think about walking straight out of it. Jenny calls something from the kitchen but it's muffled by the pan sizzling so I don't hear. I walk upstairs with my bag.

I look at her face and see it; the face that made me do this. The shape of her nose. The same colour eye shadow. Even unconscious the resemblance to my mother is uncanny.

I close the bathroom door behind me with my elbow, put on the latex gloves that are in my trouser pocket, and open the bag to reveal the plastic sheet. I lay it out in the cramped space. Kneeling on it I find a suitable place within arm's reach to lay the contents of the wash bag. From it, I take a sealed bag containing a syringe barrel and a packet with a single needle. After placing them together I take out the small bottle of clear liquid and fill the syringe with its contents. After checking for air bubbles, I place it on the edge of the bath.

I glance at my watch and lean to flush the unused toilet. I turn on the hot tap and take the overall from my bag. Once I have it on, I pick up the syringe, turn off the tap and wait.

I feel a familiar tingle within me but I am not aroused. I don't want to fuck her. I want to rob her of the body that she thinks should be hers, like she did to me.

She calls my name as she climbs the stairs. The right name this time. 'Jude. Lunch is ready. Are you OK in there?' I purposefully do not answer. She says my name again as she reaches the top of the stairs. I stand behind the door and hold my breath. She knocks gently. 'Jude, are you OK?'

My knuckles are white around the barrel of the syringe and the swishing of blood in my ears begins to make me feel dizzy. I can't hold it any longer and an explosion of breath escapes from my mouth.

The door handle begins to turn.

I've changed my mind. I am about to push the door to prevent her from entering, tell her I'm fine and head out of the front door as soon as I can when Jenny throws open the door. She sees the sheet, the instruments, and then me. She begins to scream. I know that a neighbour is home as I saw the car as I came in the back door and I panic.

As she turns to run from the bathroom, I leap forward and grab her. She is struggling and we stumble. Her screams are becoming louder and I panic. Feeling the syringe in my hand, I fall onto her and inject the ketamine where my hand lands, on her thigh.

I know that the ketamine will take four to five minutes to kick in and I need to keep her quiet until then. The injection has understandably alarmed her and the screaming continues. I quietly but firmly say her name and tell her that if she continues to scream, I will be forced to slit her throat. The threat doesn't quieten her racket. The scalpel is within my reach and while still on top of her, I grab it and pull it towards us. Getting a proper grip of it, I slide it to her throat. Breathy sobbing replaces the screams and when I am satisfied that she has stopped the screaming, I let her sit up against the bath. She looks at me, her eyes darting between me and the instruments laid out on the floor.

'What is this? What did you just inject me with?'

'I wanted to tell you the truth about me. I gave you a mild dose of tranquiliser because I was frightened that you would walk away without letting me explain everything.'

'What the fuck is everything?'

I unzip the overall and unbutton my shirt revealing my strapped torso.

Crying and visibly afraid, she stares at me as I begin to unstrap my chest. There is an audible intake of breath as my immature breasts are revealed. I unfasten my belt and unbutton the jeans, allowing them to drop.

'Before I show you, I need to explain.'

'What are you going to do to me?'

Her impatience irritates me. This is not about her. I am trying to explain and offer her a way out of this but she isn't listening. I was right to think that she is like mother.

'Please, Jenny, just listen to me. I have a condition.'

Her eyes widen.

'What condition makes you inject a woman who was falling for you with a tranquiliser, dress up like a freak and, what? What's the sheet for? Are you going to rape me? Oh God! You have breasts! Are you even a man?'

'Shut up and listen! Of course I'm a man! I have a penis!'

Her eyes drop to my underpants. She looks puzzled and rubs her eyes. At first I think she is mocking me but I soon realise that the ketamine is starting to take effect. Her speech is starting to slur. 'What is this *condition*?'

'I am a hermaphrodite. I have both male and female organs.'

I start to tell her about how my mother – the woman she represents so well, chose to bring me up as a girl. As I speak, she is fighting the effects of the tranquiliser, desperately trying to stay awake. I have only ever tried to be this honest with my mother but she always shut me down. I look to Jenny for reassurance, but the look of disgust as she succumbs to the tranquiliser tells me all I need to know. I put my clothes back on and zip up the overall, then pull Jenny onto the sheet and begin to undress her.

Goodnight, god bless, mother. Don't let the bed bugs bite.

Laurence and Numb Nuts

LEDLOWE GUTHRIE

I never liked that joker Dan Blakey. Running after Mister Laurence like a sheep dog. He don't know nothing that Dan. Look at him, right up the arse of Mister Laurence. Loz this and Loz that. Thinks he's the sidekick. Mister Laurence is alright. He's tall. Wouldn't want to get on the wrong side of him but. Might ask him for a job. Bet he's got some rubbish that wants taking to the tip. He's got plenty people working for him. You can tell by the state of his vines. Perfect neat like lines of soldiers getting smaller in the distance. I've seen them workers in the vineyards squatting down, twisting and clipping them vines. I wouldn't want to do that, in the burning sun, dry as a nun's tit.

It's 30 degrees and we're up on some platform in the middle of one of the orchards. Me, Jade, Dan Fucking Blakey and Mister Laurence. The big man's stretching out his freckled arms and grasping that wooden railing that runs around the edge of his stage. Like he's captain of his ship, sailing a sea of all purples and greens in the fields all around him. True, they are his. Not like my dad's piddly, shitty, toy town farm. From up here you can just about make out the dry row ends. He'll be thinking of the cash. Proper cocking business man, he is.

'D'you fancy a ride then, Jade?' Mister Laurence says. His legs are stretched apart. And I can see a couple of black hairs sticking out over the top of his waistband.

Jade looks a bit nervous. She's typical of the sort he likes. Pretty. Skinny arse. Some of them are gobby but not all. And I'm only here 'cos of Jade. She's sweet as. She asked me if I wanted to come.

Excited she was last night when she got back to the shed and told me Mister Laurence'd invited her to his place in the afternoon. Normally she's just hanging about reading or making some jewellery shit she's got in her room. And sometimes she talks to me. Like she did yesterday and asked if I'd come with her to this invite she'd had off of her boss. I could see she liked it. She was all pink in her cheeks so I said, 'Fuck it. Yes, I'll fucking come.'

He's got loads of Maoris working on his farm, Mister LJ, but he never invites them to his fucking little parties. Nor none of them locals with their cross eyes and bad language. He'd never mess with someone's daughter what he knew. It's these backpackers what turn up for a few weeks' work. My dad remembers him and his putting himself about from way back at school. Before all this land and factory and vineyard and shit. My dad was the little guy that no one knew and Mister Laurence Jones, without the Mister in them days, he was always the loud mouth. Always had the big ideas. Think my old man might've been jealous but.

Old LJ's got loads of glasses. Tasting glasses he says for wine tasting. Fucking obvious these jokers. Can't come up with a better name. So when Jade doesn't answer about the ride Mister Laurence says let's have a different wine and he passes a glass to old fucking numb nuts Blakey.

'This little jewel here,' he says as he's passing a glass to fucking rat-face Dan, 'is crisp and fresh like newly cut grass.' He passes one to Jade. 'What do you think of that one, sweetie?'

I get the distinct feeling Jade's not that much of a boozer. She knocks it back like a shot and I'm watching Mister Laurence holding it in his big mouth full of dazzling-white teeth and then he swills it round like he's gargling before he swallows.

I don't normally drink 'cept I might have a tinny if my little bro's friends are round playing pool in the barn. But I'm a bit pissed that Mister Laurence isn't giving me any of his jewel wine.

'I'll have a glass of that,' I say and clock Mister Laurence lifting his eyebrows at Numb Nuts.

He smiles at me cos Mister Laurence is like that. He's a smiler. Wants everyone to like him. 'Sorry Roy,' he says. 'Didn't realise.' And he pours something out of a jug into a glass

I can see it's fucking water. He must think I'm an idiot. 'I'm not having no water,' I say. 'I want that.' And him and Half-eaten Pasty Face Dan do that dirty look at each other again.

'Oh sorry, mate,' says Mister LJ, 'I didn't know you liked wine.'

Fucking liar.

He pours me a glass and hands it and I neck it. Hold my glass out for another. Mister LJ shrugs and fills it up.

'You like it then, Roy? Got a taste for the good stuff, eh?'

I neck it again and hold the glass out, smiling at him. I see this look like he's not sure now. Am I taking the piss?

He holds the bottle up and squints into the sun. It's beating down and his nice white shirt's got dark bits under the arms. 'Last drop, Roy. You're lucky.' He pours a few dribbles into my glass then straight off opens another bottle for him and Numb Nuts who's sitting nice and open like his balls are on fire

I look at Jade see what she's doing and she's holding out her glass for Mister Laurence. Her eyes are all shiny and she's taken off her sandals. Mister Laurence sits down beside her. Makes her look tiny. He puts a hand on her knee and says, 'So, do you feel like a run out yet, beautiful?'

And she says, 'Can Roy come?'

I'd be well up for that. He's only got a fucking Mercedes-Benz!

We end up out by his machine.

'So this is a 1995 Mercedes-Benz SL Class 350 Sports,' he says and to be honest I'm probably the only one here paying any attention. He opens the driver's seat and strokes it. 'Nothing like leather,' he says then bends his head closer and sniffs it with his big wine farmer's nose.

Jade's just leaning on the hot paintwork making little sweat marks. Last week I saw Mister LJ, he was buying a bag of sugar at Dawn's and he said hello and all that shit and when I said I'd seen he had that nice-looking Merc he told me he'd give me a ride sometime, so I suppose he's a man of his word. Might be alright except it looks like Dan Shit Head is coming 'n'all.

Then I notice that Mister LJ and little Dan are talking very quiet for a change and looking at me and Dan's shaking his head. He's never spoken to me even though he lives along the same road. Even though he came and bought chickens off my old man. Even though my old lady nursed Dan's grandson when he had measles last year.

When snakey Dan came in the house he pretended he couldn't see me.

Eventually Mister LJ steps away and Dan says, 'Shall we go first, Jade? Me and you?'

Course Jade wants me to come along. Not as stupid as muppet Dan thought. So I sit in the back just watching and he's got his hand on her knee right after he's put it in gear. He's talking all the time, full of shit he is about how that engine could get up to 160 in 5 seconds. My arse! He's a crock of shit. Wouldn't do that in half an hour. Anyway the girl is just nodding along like she's interested, so I says 'bullshit' under my breath and Dan says, 'Alright in the back there, Roy?' I nod thinking he got the message. But then when we get a little bit along the road he turns into one of the fields and parks up in the shade under some massive trees and starts necking with the girl. Right in front of me. Just like that. All over her. Hands on her knee, up her skirt, then starts going up her t-shirt and I'm wondering what she's going to say and then she says,

'Oh, I don't think it's right with Roy here,' and pushes him off.

Well I can tell she doesn't like him, not at all, but he says,

'Roy? He's a good lad, he doesn't mind. Do you, Roy?' so I just say, 'Wanker,' and look out the window but anyway I think she's pissed on his bonfire so to speak and he turns the key in the ignition. Smooth as, that engine.

When we get back to the platform Mister Laurence has necked another bottle and he's got sweat patches all over his white shirt now. He leans down to grab Jade's hand as she's climbing up to the platform. 'I'll take you for another drive later if you feel like it, Angel,' he says. He'll be up her like a rat up a drainpipe and when Jade looks at me I can see kipper-face Dan watching her arse from behind.

'What time've you got to be home, Roy?' Mister Laurence is looking at me hard while he's handing another glass of his finest to Jade.

I shake my head. 'Got nothing on,' I say. 'I'm good as gold here.'

'How's your old man cope without you around?'

I hear cock splat Dan snigger.

'We've got it sussed right,' I say. 'He knows.' I pick up my glass again. 'I'll have another one 'n'all,' and I nod at the dripping bottle in his big brown hairy hand.

Mister LJ looks like he might be going to spit the dummy. And Jade looks like she's not far off throwing up.

Then I see his shoulders relax a bit. He comes over and fills my glass right to the top. 'Why don't you take your jacket off, Roy? You must be sweating like a pig in this heat.'

'Nah. I'm right,' I say and skull the wine. If I had a fucking choice I'd have a super but if Mister Laurence is handing it out… and it's cold. I look at Jade, she's slumped back in her chair and her eyes are near as closed. I think she'd probably be best off back in her room right now. Least if she's going to chunder it'll be in her own place.

Dan the Weasel says, 'Need a slash.' And he pulls his zip down then turns and I can hear this piss hitting the side of the platform. 'I'll not charge for watering your crops, Loz.'

Mister LJ's laugh is getting even louder and he crashes into the wooden railing. 'I'm going to take her for a drive now, mate.' And he leans over Jade and taps her head. I think he meant to stroke it.

'Don't think she's interested,' I say to the Big Man. 'But I'll go with you.'

'Don't you worry, Roy.' Mister LJ shows me his big teeth again. 'She's interested all right.'

'She's definitely up for it.' That puppet Dan nods his head like it's going to come off. 'Girls like her–'

'Why don't you stay here with Dan?' says Mister LJ. 'Here, let me top you up again, mate.' And he fills the glass. 'This is last year's.'

These two shitheads are beginning to get right on my nerves now. Couple of fucking clowns. I've heard shit going off in the bars in town. Where there's a rumour there's some kind of stink. I wouldn't trust either of them with a dead parrot.

'If Jade's going, I'm going with her,' I say and I stand up right in front of Mister swaying-like-fucking-Pisa Laurence. I'm staring straight at the curls of wet hair stuck to his chest.

'Tell you what, Roy,' he shouts, spitting a bit, 'you come back here tomorrow and me and you'll go out for a ride.' He stops and I'm not sure if he's finished but he starts pulling at Jade and tosser Dan grabs one of her hands. It's like watching a couple of retards fucking a doorknob.

Now I've not known Jade all that long. She's been living in the shed next to me in the big barn for three weeks and four days now. I like her but. She's just trying to make some money to get back to England before her visa runs out. She's had some shit going on at home with her ex she says. None of my business but I asked her why she stayed with someone for so long if he was knocking her about. She just said it was complicated. Like I say none of my business but straight up I don't know why she stayed with someone with a temper like that. Anyways I reckon that if Jade wasn't off her face with Mister LJs nice, grass-tasting wine she wouldn't be going for a ride with Mister sweaty LJ.

Jade's shaking her head and her eyes are closed. I think he's going to have to carry her if he wants to get her down the steps. And she holds her hand out towards me.

'Mister Laurence,' I say, 'any cunt can see she doesn't want your dirty dick anywhere near her.'

Both the fuckers stop and drop Jade back on her chair.

'Dirty dick?' the big man says back at me like he's deaf.

'Dirty. And I hear it's not so big neither.'

See like I said. He thinks he's the big guy. Thinks he's better than people like my dad, the little farmers. I heard stories down the tavern.

Dim Dan does a classic clenching of his fists and pulling his shoulders back, hopping around like he's in a boxing ring, fat chance of that. 'That's fighting talk that is,' he hisses at me, 'isn't it Loz?' He's got a lazy eye and when he's pissed it slides right into the corner.

Mister LJ looks like the wind went out of his sails. He looks up into the sky. It's still all clear blue and big as fuck.

'You looking for a hiding, talking to Mister Laurence Jones like that, you little shit?'

That little rat Dan couldn't give a paper bag a hiding but he edges closer to me and he's still got his glass in his hand, slopping the wine on the deck.

I'm not interested in fuck knuckle Dan. I'm concentrating on Mister Laurence Jones who ain't a stupid man but he's well drunk. And I can't see his big white smile no more. He moves towards me 'n'all and the two of them stare down at me sitting right next to Jade. I can't see their faces no more cos they've got the sun right behind them and they're all silhouette. Like Little and Large. Large is breathing heavy and swaying and Little is fidgeting like a cockroach.

Lucky for me and not so lucky for Mister Laurence he stumbles and crashes onto the floor and smacks his big nose. I can see blood on the wood as he stands up with his hand on his face trying to stop it pouring down his face and onto his not so fucking clean white shirt.

He steps back and says, through his hand, 'Well, that was the last bottle we finished up. I'm going to go and cool down back inside. Dan, shall we run through that little bit of business we were talking about finishing off?'

'Top idea, Bossman,' says dim Dan and moves away and necks what's left in his glass. Then he turns and follows Mister Laurence down the steps and they piss off back to the farm.

I look at Jade and wonder how the fuck I'm going to get her back to our place.

Of Love and Revolution in a City

TABITHA BAST

Recriminations.

The cobblestones lie uprooted on their backs like beetles. The windows of the banks and the Renaissance hotel are still boarded up. Alongside the silver-tongued porter at the Renaissance stands a scrum of police, their jackets strained across their enormous backs. They are brothers bearing the same shoulders, flat faces and cropped hair; same posture. They stand close with hips and guns pointed towards each other. He stands away from them, uneasy. I imagine him chewing at his lip, like me, enlivened with suspicion and fear. My mouth is ulcerated, my tongue swollen from my own treacherous teeth. I pick at my lips and they split and bleed.

My eyes are dry like the plants I forgot to water. My eyes and the plants have lost their green and are turning brown. Together. It is autumn. I can see the park from here, a little park, with little people, walking their little dogs, the little trees are turning their leaves over, growing weary of life and faltering in the winds. In the knowledge that winter is coming.

I won't think on to winter without him, or that he is without blankets, handcuffed in the naked cell asleep on his feet. I don't think whether he is turning colour, weary. Or of how many broken bones it will take to break his silence. Or how many days before they come for me.

I'm lying. Of course I think, how many?

Revolution is just mathematics. We try to multiply, they subtract us, divide us, fractions, fractures. Numbers possess me now. Just 4 days, 11 hours since I last saw him, x nights and y days until he is safe. Algebra, arithmetic. Scant substitute for simple counting. Him and me make two.

A knocking of knuckles at the door. My body spasms although my mind is crisp like the morning air, cold and bright up on the park and the police and the doorman. The knock is soft and shy, our neighbour from downstairs. Her eyes kissed with absinth that she drinks from a teacup since her son disappeared and she broke all her glasses. Her tongue swollen with the edge that is her nerves. We all wear our tongues wide and big this season; me, the neighbour, the doorman, the little people in the little park.

She taps again, a little rougher. I give in because I am weak and because she has a key anyway. I call out to her without lifting my eyes from the window, 'Let yourself in,' and the door eases open, unlocked before I had spoken.

Here she is with her coat on for all the trees are shedding theirs. She pulls a parcel like a weapon from under her arm, the substance I've been forgetting, the food I won't think to buy now. She loves me from her long-lived distance. Sometimes I consider hugging her, I appreciate this neighbour for all her dull stories, her moral lecturing, her recriminations.

'Don't let them take your hunger from you,' she prescribes, unwrapping bread and cheese to fry, two large eggs. She has invited herself to join the meal. 'I feel for you. I do.' We both think of her son – annoyance for me and reward for her. I nod. The doorman patrols up and down a few paces, like a caged puma. He walks, two paces left, two right, repeats, jailed like the rest of us, even the free ones.

'Will you cook for me?' I ask her. 'I want to see if he will return…'

'Of course he will,' she scoffs. 'This was a riot not a revolution.' says the woman who has witnessed enough to know the difference. 'And neither are worth the loss.'

I swear at her and she shrugs and shuffles into the kitchen. Her leg is arthritic. I have no regrets. Not this morning when I feel strictly alive. My eyes have dried and my fingers are peeling because they haven't touched him for so long. The chaos that is my belly burns me up. But in my discomfort I feel potent.

When the phone yelps I know it's not him. It's not. It is Federica, I recognise her rural accent at once. She sounds tired. We are all tired, awake too long, stretching out the hours and the day, as if this sacrifice, this martyrdom, can salvage it all. We are worker bees, making hope instead of honey. She tells me of a prisoner solidarity march highlighting the abuses and demanding their release. This evening we will march on the jail, like bats carried forth on the vibrations of our loved ones. Or sheep, lambs bleating our misery as they pick more of us off.

I am foolish, the neighbour is right. No loss is worth it. The loss of me to them so as to register my pointless protest, it is not worth it. But I am going anyway, if only because prisoners might hear us. If only for feeling the love of friends around me. If only because a lone guard might be going home unheeded. If only because to sit here and listen to that clock is tearing me apart as violently as any truncheon.

So. I forfeit my vigil to return to the streets, re-dressing in black, more a widow spider than a wailing one, and I see myself, in the chipped mirror in the wardrobe. I see myself and I stop.

'It looks good on you.' the neighbour comments kindly, nodding to my head, she thinks I have dyed it. My hair, once black, has turned red, just as my mother teased me. *All the rage in this young girl's head will colour her good black locks.*

These winds must have changed. A rush, like whisky, brings life to cold toes. The neighbour passes me coffee, reminding me that food is ready. I dress and drink; no time to ponder miracles although I snatch looks at the mirror unabashed in front of the old lady.

'Where are you going now?' she clucks disapprovingly. 'Dressed for war not peace.'

'Both.' I retort testily, pulling a scarf over my new appearance, not wishing to be a beacon to a baton.

In the kitchen, I sit to eat, pushing bread in mouth and boots on feet.

'Stay here for if he calls?' I plead, knowing she will, she wants to be of service, too fragile to risk the demonstrations herself. She is behind us, if not for us, for her boy they disappeared, breaking him and her together.

'Tell him what words? His hard-hearted loved one is out making trouble again?' she grumbles with pleasure.

She called me the loved one. A virgin acknowledgment despite her horror at our unwedded bliss. I smile and reach out and hug her. It is in revolutions that revolutions are born. I stretch out inside my armour, lowering my headscarf to conceal my raging hair. I say goodbye, carrying the last of my meal in my hand. Of all this; with burning cars and street battles and unrest and disappearances, it is a rushed breakfast which upsets her most.

Happenings
The cobblestones are being uprooted, dragged from graves like Lazarus. Evening is coming and we are growing less safe and less sane. We are near the Renaissance hotel, up at the good end of town. I live near here now, on the margins of the poor area, just on the wrong side of the invisible border.

The police have allowed us this far; we passed my street unbothered. But here the lines are growing thicker. The rumours of tanks are becoming more frequent. We have been gassed already, my skin prickles with its heat, and my clothes are damp. They started using antiquated water cannons earlier but we were at the side, unaffected.

His face was red, puffy from the gas. We watched the jet from the white cannon and he laughed. His skin is glowing, toxic, he arouses me in this state, when I tell him so he kisses me through our t-shirt sleeve masks and shouts that I am inappropriate.

We are here in this moment. Hungry and half asleep and serenely calm. When their lines dart forward to baton charge we move back but don't run, keeping footing in the hysterical crowd. There is a woman dressed in yellow screaming and weeping.

With the crowd spread and police lines retreating I catch sight of friends. I pull him by the wrist through the throng before it tightens and we are trapped on the other side. This mass, the bodies closing ranks slowly, unsure, scenting the air with the collective anticipation.

Federica spots us first, spots him first. She was once his lover. She is tall with a cleft foot like the devil, but beautiful. My lover likes her completely; everybody does, even me, although I am jealous. He and Federica were before us, long ago, before I was in his life.

This is not now. She greets us equally and then little Marko turns from his conversation, his mask keeps slipping downward. I think of children in their parent's clothes. Marko is rushed, his forehead tensed fretfully. Federica is completely covered, even her eyes concealed. I cannot see her but she still seems perturbed.

'They're bringing in guns, they're going to shoot.' His voice trembles.

'We've heard the rumour a few times today,' Federica, cynically and cold, 'not from anywhere reliable.' She is furious with her brother, I shrug it off, believing the guns and the tanks when I see them. She shouldn't have brought him; he is too young to be here.

Uproar amongst the crowd, a long legged man bounding with a stick; a police van with its front window smashed and the police pouring out, so many they must have been sitting on each other's laps. We recognise this unmasked man. We surge forward to close behind him, to take the swing of the batons on our limbs so he can escape. My lover digs his nails through my clothes so I look at him immediately, leans down to say he is going to get him somewhere safe, down these streets that we know well. And then he is gone and I am in the front line to welcome the pursuers, my arms linked with Federica and some stranger. I love them both, all faithful to each other in these moments of danger. We move forward together as if we were born together, joined like this, in congregation.

It is true about the tanks and the guns, but they don't bring them for hours and by then I know he is taken. We look for him everywhere, circling the groups, relishing the fresh water cannon that makes the crowd disperse so we can view better. But I know he has gone. A friend reports that two people were seen being arrested a street down from here, fitting his description and the one he was helping. We carry on the search half-heartedly, parting then meeting up, unwilling to be alone for long now. And then a voice:

'They're bringing in soldiers. Move back together, don't run, don't run…' Despite the words offered with such authority, some people near me start screaming, pushing outward, one heavy man falling over, some foreigner yelling in English, a hand comes in front of me and grasps their friends, plunging me backward and away from mine. The people are scattering, as light as dandelion seeds, led away in different directions leaving these streets underfoot dangerous places to stand. I move back too, into bigger shadows, slip home on the rain falling upon the cobblestones like a baptism that never ends.

Happy Harpies

MIRIAM BURKE

Helena Molony stood proudly on the cobbled stones outside Liberty Hall with four hundred women and men, waiting for the revolution to begin. She was wearing a Sam Browne belt with a pistol over her lavender cardigan and grey tweed skirt; the women were wearing civilian clothes so they could carry despatches without arousing suspicion. She hadn't slept and her body vibrated like a plucked string when a man standing near her shouted a greeting to a friend. She was disappointed not to be going with James Connolly and the other leaders to the GPO but pleased she was assigned to the detachment headed by her friend and fellow Abbey actor, Captain Seán Connolly. When Seán told her they were going to take Dublin Castle, the centre of British power for seven hundred years, she was thrilled at the daringness of it.

Helena stood at the head of nine young women, all armed with pistols. They wore knapsacks packed with food provisions and first aid kits. The women stood behind a group of twenty men, with Seán Connolly at the front. The men were armed with rifles and some were in military uniform and others wore whatever green clothes they could find or borrow. They couldn't keep their limbs still; they moved their rifles from one side to another, they adjusted their ammunition belts, they changed the tilt of their hats. The men and women of the Irish Citizen Army knew they were about to play their part in the great drama of Irish history.

At last, the order to march was given by Commandant James Connolly and the detachments set off in different directions to carry out their missions. Seán led his men and women across the steel swivel bridge that took them over the Liffey into Burgh Quay. The Corn Exchange looked alert in the spring sunshine, as if it was paying close attention to the unfolding drama. When they reached Westmoreland Street, they had to pass through crowds who had come out to feel the sun on their faces that Easter Monday. The citizens of Dublin stared at the little group of armed men and women with mild curiosity, some of them recognised Séan Connolly and Helena Molony from Abbey productions and assumed the group were rehearsing a play. No one felt fearful because men and women in rebel uniforms had been marching around the streets of Dublin for months. And James Connolly had been posting messages on a blackboard outside Liberty Hall every evening saying there would be an attack on this or that area of the city the following day.

When Captain Séan Connolly's detachment was walking along College Green, Helena heard a man in front of her whisper to his friend: 'We'll be slaughtered, Tony.'

'And it'll be our privilege,' she shouted at him.

He smiled at her and said: 'That's why I'm here.' He meant it and Helena felt guilty for shouting at him.

At the end of Dame Street, they turned left into Cork Hill, and walked across the cobbled stones towards the grey stone arch that provided a gated entrance to Dublin Castle. The 18th-century red brick buildings on either side of the gate were symbols of foreign rule. An unarmed policeman, Constable James O'Brien, was standing in front of the entrance to The Castle, and an armed soldier stood in a sentry box behind the open gate. Constable O'Brien was surprised when he saw Séan Connolly leading his group towards the arch; he had assumed they were out on a drilling exercise, and he expected them to carry on towards Lord Edward Street. When Séan reached the stone arch, he tried to go through the gate and Constable O'Brien put out an arm to stop him. Séan quickly lifted his pistol and shot James O'Brien in the head. The Constable fell to the ground and the rebels gathered around him, staring at the mess of blood and brain tissue on the side of his head. They had never seen a bullet wound. Séan shouted: 'Get in, get in. For God's sake, get in.' He was nodding at the entrance to The Castle. But they were too late; the soldier in the sentry box had closed the gate. They had lost their chance to take The Castle.

'Retreat to City Hall,' shouted Séan. 'Follow me. Quick. Run for it, run.' The soldier was shooting at them from behind the locked gate.

Helena ran after the others, weighed down by her pistol, her ammunition and the heavy knapsack.

The side entrance to City Hall was only a few feet from the gate to The Castle and Séan had a key because he worked there as a clerk. They took shelter behind the four grey stone columns in the portico while Séan struggled to fit the key in the lock; he couldn't stop his hands shaking. Helena wanted to help him but she held back.

The rebels stood for a few seconds in the great Rotunda, stunned by the ornately decorated dome, the twelve majestic fluted columns and the polished white and black marble floor.

'I want some men to guard the doors and the rest of us will shoot at The Castle from the roof. The women will set up the first aid station and take the provisions to the kitchen,' shouted Séan. The building was for him a prison where he had been trapped in a demeaning job.

When the women were walking towards the wide stone stairs, Jinny Shanahan turned to Helena Molony and whispered: 'What does that mean?' She was nodding at a mosaic on the floor with the embedded words *Obedientia Civium Urbis Felicitas*.

Helena looked at the inscription and laughed. 'It says: Happy the City Where Citizens Obey.'

'Happy The City Where the Citizens Are Free,' said Jinny.

'We'll have it changed,' said Helena. 'We'll change everything.'

Jinny looked up at the gold leaf in the ceiling and said: 'I've never seen anything so beautiful.'

'We'll turn it into flats,' said Helena.

Jinny laughed and followed her up the stairs.

The women set to work making roast beef sandwiches and tea in the kitchen.

'I can't stop thinking about the policeman,' said Jinny. She and Helena were standing next to each other buttering bread.

'I know,' said Helena.

'I recognised him - he lived in Stoneybatter. He was a Limerick man. He wasn't armed, was he?'

'Think of what they did to us during the Lock-Out,' said Helena. 'And remember the people killed on Bachelors Walk.'

'You're right. It's just that I've never seen a person die like that before. I wanted to say an Act of Contrition in his ear but it was too dangerous. Maybe we should say one now; it might still count.'

'Yes,' said Helena. 'You lead us.'

'O my God, I am heartily sorry for having offended Thee, and I detest my sins above every other evil…'

When they'd finished praying, they continued their work in silence.

The young rebel guarding the front door of City Hall heard a loud banging on the door.

'Who's there?' he asked, with his rifle cocked. He pictured an entire regiment of the British Army on the other side. He was afraid his legs were going to buckle.

'It's Kathleen Lynn.'

The young man unlocked the door and Kathleen Lynn entered the building, carrying a medical bag. Kathleen wore her dark hair in braids across the top of her head and she had round wire spectacles. She seemed unaware of the bullets falling like hailstones from the roofs behind her. The sight of her smiling face calmed the young man.

'It's good to see you, Dr Lynn. Do you have any news?'

'No, I was delivering medical supplies to the different detachments before they set off.'

'We couldn't take The Castle. There weren't enough of us.'

'Any casualties?'

'Not on our side.'

'Good. Is Helena Molony here?'

'She's in the kitchen; I'll take you there.'

'It might be best if you don't leave the door unguarded, Corporal.'

'You're right, Captain Lynn.'

When Helena saw Kathleen, she rushed over to her and said: 'I'm so glad you're with us. Any news?'

'No, I left before anything started. You had trouble at The Castle?'

'Yes, they locked the gate before we could get in.'

'It was built to withstand attacks. Do you have a first aid station?'

'I'll take you there. Would you like a cup of tea and a sandwich?'

'I'll wait until I've checked the station. The fire from The Castle is intense; we're going to have casualties.'

'I know.'

While Kathleen was unpacking bottles of morphine and field dressings, Helena asked: 'Where's Madeleine?'

'She's gone to Stephen's Green with Constance and Margaret Skinnider. Michael Mallin is their Commandant.'

'She'll be alright if she's with Constance.'

'We can only hope and pray.'

'What about Elizabeth O'Farrell and Julia?'

'They went with James and the other leaders to the GPO.'

'Julia will be relieved they're together.'

'I'm not sure it's a good thing. She'll be…'

They were interrupted by Séan Connolly who rushed into the room.

'Welcome, Captain Lynn. I'm glad you got here safely.' He turned to Helena and said: 'I need to get a message to the GPO. Will you take it?'

'Yes.'

He put out his hand and touched her arm. She was the member of his detachment he least wanted to lose – they were good friends, and she was the one he trusted most to deliver the despatches.

'I'll draw a map of the safest route. I know where the other detachments are located.'

'Good.'

While Séan drew the map, Helena turned to Kathleen and said: 'There are two letters in my knapsack.'

'I'll make sure they're delivered.'

'Thank you Kathleen.'

Helena took off her Sam Brown belt and put the pistol under the waist of her skirt. 'I once played a French governess in a farce so I'll imagine I'm playing her again when I'm out there. If I'm stopped, I'll say *I am governess from France for les enfants of the Lord Lieutenant, Baron Wimborne. I search for les croissants.*' She delivered the last two sentences in an atrocious French accent.

Kathleen laughed.

Séan handed Helena the map and the despatches. She rolled the despatches into a small tube, took the pins out of the bun at the nape of her neck, hid the despatches in her long blonde hair, and arranged her hair in another bun.

'I've asked them for more men and more ammunition. There are hundreds of soldiers getting into The Castle from Ship Street - they're beyond our range.'

'I'll give it to James myself,' said Helena.

'God Bless you, Helena. I'll take you to a door on the east side.'

Helena and Kathleen held each other tight without saying anything.

When Helena was out in the street, she forgot about Séan's map and she started running along the quickest route she knew to the GPO. She soon found herself in a doorway on a deserted street where bullets were smashing shop windows and car windscreens. She couldn't see the snipers but they seemed to be everywhere. A black and white terrier lay dead on the footpath and she could hear a child screaming in an upstairs room.

'Not now, not here, not like this,' she whispered. 'Not so soon, before I've done anything. Not alone, left on the street to die like a dog.'

There was no lull in the shooting. The street had a strategic value; it was on the way to The Castle. The rebel snipers were trying to stop troops reaching The Castle and the army were trying to kill the rebels. The shooting was not going to stop. She would be caught in the cross fire if she went into the street. She was trapped.

The garrison in City Hall would be doomed if she didn't let James Connolly know they needed reinforcements. But she couldn't deliver the message if she were lying dead in the street. Going back was no less dangerous than going forward. Nothing in her training had prepared her for this. She looked around for help but she couldn't see anyone. The shop behind her was locked and deserted. No one would risk opening a door in case they were shot. She knew she couldn't stand the noise of the gunfire for much longer. She had never felt so alone.

She remembered the lunch at Kathleen's when Kathleen told her she was too young to die. She thought of Ella and wished she was lying safe in her arms. If Constance was with her, she'd know what to do. Constance would shoot her way out.

She went down on her knees and prayed to a God she had long

neglected. And she prayed to her dead mother, asking her for protection. When she had finished, she raised one knee to stand again but before she raised the other knee, she shouted: 'That's it – that's what I'll do.'

She knelt again, put her hands on the ground, and slowly crawled out of the doorway, keeping her head low.

Boots

ELIZABETH WOODGATE

It was raining. The cars on the high street made a sound like a whip struck on a piece of leather.

'Right!' his mother said, her voice tight.

She was not in her element here, out shopping on a busy Saturday. The traffic was utterly bloody, she said. The business of parking hellish, being jostled on the pavement a ghastly ordeal and as for people not wearing gloves, well, that was the final insult. Polite society was doomed. He could feel the tension in her, crackling round her small determined shape, her pointed matronly bosom (could he even bring himself to name that part of her anatomy?) jutting out into the oncoming hordes like an aggressive piece of armour. She was always ready for a fight: with him, his father, his grandfather, shop assistants, parking attendants. And now they were going to fight about shoes. He wanted Chelsea boots, the kind The Beatles had been wearing for a few years. The fashion had even reached his school, but for his mother, this was anathema. Boots, she had said with a wrinkled brow and nose. Boots?

'Men – gentlemen – wear shoes, with laces.' She snapped out this pronouncement as she pulled open the door to Ellistons, the department store where he had been fitted for school uniform for the last twelve years. Only two more to go now, but these two years were filled with the possibility of meeting girls at the dances the school laid on. 'Joining forces' was the phrase his housemaster used to describe the Saturday evening rituals where boys lined up against one wall and girls against another. 'The opposition' the upper years always called them, as though they were there to play rugger, not do the twist. They came from neighbouring establishments, ones like his, with rows of iron beds like some Dickensian nightmare, but with girls in them, not boys.

When he'd first seen the iron beds, fourteen of them it must have been, all in the same room, a small bedside cupboard separating each one, he'd wanted to scream, or cry or be sick. But he'd done none of these things, just felt a punch in his gut, possibly his solar plexus – wherever that was – and this feeling had lingered all that first term: a dull ache of horror at being left in such a grey, cold, regimented place.

It had become less regimented, of course. He'd stopped noticing the iron bed frames after a bit, the anonymity of those uniform spaces became familiar and individual: Johnson in the space next to him that first year, announcing he was awake every morning with a trumpeting fart; Trent-Smith on his other side, who had what seemed like a never ending supply of ginger nuts from his tuck box. And the atmosphere of the room, so still and empty when he'd first experienced it, filled up with filthy jokes – getting filthier as the years went on – with banter, mild bullying, a hoard of swear words and nicknames that became a separate language, a dialect that could never be used, understood even, with adults, at home, in the classroom.

But now that he was going into the sixth form, the dormitory days were over. He had been made a junior prefect and with that honour came the privilege of a study bedroom, shared with only one other. Along with this privacy, and the relief of being able to choose subjects he actually quite liked, came the opportunity to be more individual when it came to dress. From the beginning of his time there, he'd been watching the boys in the top two years. The interesting ones, the ones who looked as though they knew there was a life to be lived outside the prison walls of a boarding school, grew their hair longer, had sideburns that reached to their jaws if they were lucky enough for their hormones to have kicked in, had trousers that were narrow, and boots, not shoes.

Boots.

That was the deal. You needed boots. Boots that were made for walking, dancing, getting the hell out of there.

But his mother was in charge, she reminded him with every impatient gesture, raise of her eyebrow, tut of her tongue against her teeth. His father did not get involved with clothing dilemmas. He paid the bills, went through the cheque book stubs, serviced the car, mowed the lawn and stayed firmly at work, for as long as possible. Safer that way. No need then to get tangled up in domestic squabbling. He let his wife reign supreme. And of course he wore shoes. Always. The only boots he possessed were wellingtons and the leather climbing ones he kept in the boot of his car, along with a tin of dubbin and a soft cloth.

Now they had reached the men's shoe department, and a display at the front featured exactly the pair of boots he'd set his heart on. She might, just might, be won over. If he could have buttered her up, he would. 'Turning on the charm', Johnson called it. But he just didn't know what to say.

'Your hair looks nice today, Mum.' Would that work?

But her hair was arranged in its usual helmet of curls, brushed away from her forehead so that the frown lines and grey hairs creeping along her temples were clearly on show and did not look nice. He couldn't pat her on the shoulder, hold her hand as he'd done before he went to prep school. When was the last time they'd touched each other? He had no idea. Certainly not this holidays.

'May I be of service, madam?' The shop assistant was creepy rather than charming, but his mother responded with a smile of relief as though someone had offered to lift a heavy bag off her arm.

'My son.' She gestured at him to sit down. 'He needs measuring. He seems to have been growing.' She paused and gave a laugh. 'Again!'

He could feel his skin turn hot and he wanted to reach out and grab the back of her head and slam her forehead against the poster on the wall that showed a James Bond type smoothie in some shiny black shoes and a dark suit. The kind of man his mother probably wanted him to turn into.

His long thin foot, exposed in its grey sock, measured a twelve, the shop assistant intoned. A whole size bigger than last year.

'Twelve!' His mother laughed again. 'Heavens! Have you anything that will fit? It's for school. He needs to look smart.'

The assistant gave him a brief glance. There was something about his mouth that seemed familiar. The way one incisor overlapped his central tooth almost at right angles.

'I'll bring a selection, madam.'

'Boots?' He mouthed over his shoulder so that his mother wouldn't see.

'If you'd like to come with me, sir.'

His mother looked up from the glove she was manoeuvring off her fingers in a series of sharp tugs.

'Make sure you bring something suitable.'

'Of course, madam.'

The assistant showed his incisor again and then he remembered where he'd seen it. At the pub, the one time he'd made it this summer without his parents realising. They'd been out at some do and Nick, his friend from prep school, had invited him to chance it even though they were still two years away from drinking legally. Two pubs chucked them out before they got lucky. Nick had got hold of some fags and this was their bargaining tool. They'd approached a group on their way in and offered them a packet of Number 6 in exchange for getting them a pint. Incisor had been the friendliest.

'Yeah, all right, mate,' he'd said. 'My brother used to do that for me when I was your age. But you'd better go through into the garden and make sure the barman doesn't see you.'

And now here they were again. He didn't have any fags to offer but he did have some money on him.

'Have a pint on me, mate,' he said, digging half a crown out of his pocket.

Incisor grinned.

'Thank you kindly, young sir.'

At the end of an hour, the only pair that the assistant deemed to be a proper fit were a pair of narrow, high ankle boots. They weren't as pointed as he'd hoped and the leather was too shiny, but he'd soon knock the crap out of them.

His mother, her mouth a thin line, was writing a cheque at the counter. The assistant was smiling but his mother would not meet anyone's eye.

'Boots,' she said, as they walked down the street. 'If your

housemaster complains, you'll just have to say they were the only things we could find to fit your enormous feet.'

He grinned down at her shoulders as he walked one step behind her, his mind already so many steps ahead.

Three Conversations with Mr Sienkiewicz

JONATHAN HOLLAND

Edward has always been fascinated by the homeless people he sometimes sees about. He wonders how it's possible to grow up and become an adult, and to have some kind of life behind you, whilst still remaining as alone as Edward himself feels for much of the time, at age thirteen and despite all the people in his life.

It was a couple of years ago that he first saw Mr Sienkiewicz in Victoria Park. He was not especially keen to get back home to an empty house. He still sometimes stops on his way back from school to sit and maybe do a drawing, maybe read one of his Dad's dozens of books, which he's slowly working his way through as he promised he would before his Dad died. Mr Sienkiewicz was there often, and on a couple of occasions that Edward's been in the park with his mum, she'd pointed him out, always there in the same spot on the bench on the other side of the fence.

'Where does he sleep?' Edward asks, and his mum replies that she didn't know. In summer, perhaps he sleeps in the open air or in the tunnel next to the railway station; she's seen them down there. *Them*, as she refers to homeless people. Edward wonders whether losing your home transforms people in this way, from being us to being them. In the winter, his mother explains, the council's probably set something up. Come to think of it, there are local churches, St Peter's for example, which open their doors to the homeless. He'll be all right, he'll survive. But Edward is not so sure, because surviving is not what being all right means.

His mum has told him once or twice not to speak to the homeless man, and when Edward asks why not, she speaks of something she's heard from the other mothers. This has made Mr Sienkiewicz an object of great fascination to Edward. Other questions, such as what Mr Sienkiewicz eats, how old he is, whether he's mad, whether he can have showers, and what he does when he's ill, are met by his mum with similarly vague responses.

'Poland, maybe,' she'd said when he asks where he's from. 'Romania. Somewhere like that.'

Edward parks his Raleigh. Mr Sienkiewicz is sitting there on his bench opposite the swings, just beyond the fence, looking as though he's been half wrapped up by someone and then left behind, perhaps forgotten altogether. He's plump and puffy-eyed, with a small amount of matted white hair, and he gives the impression that he'd be rough to the touch even in his smooth places. The lower portion of Mr Sienkiewicz's face is part-covered by a brown woollen scarf, his hands pushed deep inside his overcoat pockets, and next to him on the bench there is a large plastic bottle of something called White Ace.

Moving with great slowness, Mr Sienkiewicz withdraws one of his hands, looks up and beckons Edward over with a raised, tubby finger.

'My mum told me not to talk to you,' Edward says, aware that with these very words, he's failing to comply with that request.

'I watch you,' Mr Sienkiewicz says. 'I come here to watch the children.' Considering the enormous vessel of a body in which it's housed, his voice is surprisingly high-pitched and gentle. He closes his eyes tight shut and then opens them again, so widely that a spark seems to flash from them, and he smiles.

'Are you a paedophile?' Edward asks, feeling that this would be useful information to have before proceeding. Mr Sienkiewicz does not reply to this, but screws up his eyes and stares hard at Edward, who finds that he is suddenly transfixed: he could watch Mr Sienkiewicz all afternoon, with his weird expressions and his funny way of speaking. This is despite his smell: the longer you stand there, you realize that Mr Sienkiewicz sometimes uses himself as a toilet. Which probably, Edward thinks, has its advantages if you have no home.

Edward is a method-minded lad: the description of him, delivered during a chat with his mother about his lack of progress, comes from Mrs Starling, who followed it with the phrase 'but not a particularly bright one'. He proceeds to ask Mr Sienkiewicz about the things he doesn't know about him, but Mr Sienkiewicz's answers are not always clear and Edward has to fill in some of the missing bits. When Edward asks what Mr Sienkiewicz eats, the reply is 'food: we all have equal stomachs', his English suddenly and strangely perfect. To the question about whether he has showers, Mr Sienkiewicz tells him it's not easy for him to do that.

Then Mr Sienkiewicz seems to fall asleep for about ten minutes, uttering some Polish words half-way through. When he wakes up, Edward, who's taken the chance to draw a quick sketch of Mr Sienkiewicz's head, asks what he does when he falls ill. Mr Sienkiewicz says he used to go to the doctor, but now he doesn't bother so much: he points at his fat legs and what look like fat ankles. He is 73 years old, he says, but at the moment he can't remember when his birthday is.

'It might be today, then,' Edward says, 'September 17th. Happy birthday.'

At this Mr Sienkiewicz's eyes crinkle in what remains of his smile. 'You ask many questions,' he says. 'This is good.'

'Do you sleep in a church?'

'Sometimes yes. In a church doorway, in a hostel, in the park. Sometimes yes, sometimes no. All the time I am tired.'

'Are you mad?' Edward wonders. 'Everybody looks at you and thinks that you are. That's my final question, you'll be pleased to hear.'

'For them I am mad,' Mr Sienkiewicz says, not specifying who 'them' is, but Edward knows. 'You. Do you think I am mad?'

'I don't know yet. You're a bit hard to understand, but that doesn't mean you're mad. Where are you from?'

'Excuse me,' a woman says who's suddenly appeared. 'Are you alright?' Edward and Mr Sienkiewicz slowly turn towards the unwelcome interrupter, whose voice is loud. Neither is clear who she's speaking to, but it's Edward she's looking at.

'Yes, thanks,' he says.

'Well, if he's bothering you, love, we're over there.' Over there is a short line of formidable mothers who all seem to have their arms folded.

'Actually,' Edward explains, 'I'm the one bothering him.'

'I am harmless,' Mr Sienkiewicz says to her. 'Look at me. I am old, fat. I am no bother. Look.' But her expression shows the woman remains unconvinced: turning to leave, she offers the opinion that a play area is no place for him. '*Pieprzona suka*,' says Mr Sienkiewicz when she's gone. Edward repeats the sound, and Mr Sienkiewicz smiles, pleased.

Still in no rush to get home, because as well as it being an empty house there are equations to be done, Edward hops over the fence and sits down on the bench next to Mr Sienkiewicz. There is something about him that urges Edward to learn more, despite Mr Sienkiewicz just having issued a weapons-grade fart: sparrows flutter from a tree, wisely escaping the area.

Although he knows now what a homeless person does, Edward doesn't know what Mr Sienkiewicz is actually like, and Mr Sienkiewicz, who seems happy enough looking at the children, sitting there fatly breaking wind and smiling gently, doesn't seem in any hurry to tell him. He's a mystery, Mr Sienkiewicz is, a potent-smelling mystery wrapped in rags. Looking around him at the mothers and fathers, the children, the dogs, Edward works out that he already knows about them, where they go, what they watch, how they spend their lives, because their lives aren't so very different from his own, i.e. tedious and governed by the wishes of others, something you'd want to escape from.

But about the real Mr Sienkiewicz, the man Mr Sienkiewicz had been before he lost his home and perhaps also himself, Edward knows nothing. And what's more, being from a foreign country, he's homeless twice over: let's not, Edward tells himself, forget that.

Edward wishes to know how Mr Sienkiewicz has come to be here, homeless in Victoria Park in September, and asks him, adding 'It doesn't matter if you don't want to tell me.'

'I do not know,' Mr Sienkiewicz replies, 'how I came to be here. And also, I will not tell you. You are a boy.' He reaches over, raises the plastic bottle to his lips with a heavy arm that trembles slightly, and drinks. 'Mine,' he states, 'is the usual story.'

'How long have you been in England?' asks Edward.

'Fifteen years, twenty maybe. Why are you asking me these questions? Now you are making me tired with your fucking questions.'

'A school project,' Edward says. 'They asked us to find a homeless person and interview him.'

'That is a lie,' Mr Sienkiewicz declares, and Edward agrees that it is, that his teachers spend all their time making people aware that the world is in a mess but without showing them what to do about it. 'Gdansk,' Mr Sienkiewicz says, 'is where I was from.' Edward asks him to spell that, and Mr Sienkiewicz does. Noting that Mr Sienkiewicz's words are suddenly not coming out of his mouth properly, he asks for a repetition, but confusingly the letters come out in a different order this time, and they have to spend some time working it out.

'I asked my mum what to give homeless people,' Edward says in a little speech he's prepared for when the time comes, which is now. 'Because she says not to give money because they spend it on stuff like that stuff in the bottle. So I went on Google and found a list of the things that homeless people need.' On the list had been socks and shoes, blankets, toiletries and high-calorie food. But these people aren't called *sockless* or *toiletries-less* people, they are *homeless*. What they need is right there in their name, but people don't see it.

'I'm Edward,' Edward says, and holds out his hand, which he feels is an appropriate action, given what he's about to do. Mr Sienkiewicz observes the hand for a moment before refusing, perhaps thinking it would be too great an effort to lean forward and reach out. Clearly used to parcelling out his energies, he raises instead his bottle to his lips.

'Edward,' he says, and burps slightly and sighs. 'In Polish, *Edzio*. Repeat that.'

'Edzio,' says Edward, slightly startled.

'Edzio. My name is Sienkiewicz. I changed it, but now I am Sienkiewicz again.'

'Please could you say that again?'

'Sien-kie-wicz.'

'Thanks,' Edward says. He tears out the page on which he's drawn Mr Sienkiewicz's head: Mr Sienkiewicz doesn't seem like the kind of person who'd have WhatsApp or Google Maps, or indeed know what they were at all. 'Our address is written on the back.

Mine and my mum's. Come whenever you want, Mr Sienkiewicz. Except Saturday mornings when we're at Tesco's. It's over there.' He points towards the general area of 37 Rainow Road and Mr Sienkiewicz slowly swivels his head half an inch in the same direction as the number of furrows in his brow subtly increases. He takes the piece of paper and pockets it without removing his eyes from Edward's. God only knows what other items are to be found at the bottom of that pocket. There might be small, dead animals in there.

'Thank you,' he murmurs. '*Dziękuję.*'

'I could sleep on the sofa for a bit. You can't stay forever, though,' Edward warns Mr Sienkiewicz. 'There has to be a limit. And also, you shouldn't drink that stuff, Mr Sienkiewicz.'

Shortly before the park gates are to be closed for the night, a bearded policeman approaches them and asks them to leave. Mr Sienkiewicz refuses, gesturing with his fat arms, saying he's on the other side of the fence from the play area. Spit flies from his mouth as he stands, and he's breathing heavily. The policeman insists, wondering whether Edward doesn't have a home to go to: he places a gloved hand on Mr Sienkiewicz's arm, but Mr Sienkiewicz shakes it off, angrily saying something in Polish.

'He's telling you,' Edward tells the policeman, 'to fuck off. I speak Polish. He's asking what harm he's doing. Why can't he stay?' But in the end the policeman leads Mr Sienkiewicz away, very slow and unsteady on his feet, towards the doorway of a church perhaps, towards a tunnel, or a bridge. The bearded policeman will at some point walk away towards somewhere he belongs, and Edward imagines Mr Sienkiewicz standing there, leaning against a lamppost, uncertain about where to turn and anyway finding it a struggle to do so, with his weight, and the White Ace overpowering his senses.

Over the following days, Mr Sienkiewicz does not reappear. Edward asks his mum what 'the usual story' means when it came to homeless people. It might be a series of unfortunate events coming together, she explains, after being annoyed that he'd been talking to Mr Sienkiewicz: losing your job, family problems, having nowhere to go. Perhaps Mr Sienkiewicz has a family back in Poland, but perhaps they've fallen out of touch, or they're not speaking, or something.

That happens in families more than you'd think. It's awful, really, when you think about it.

His face glowing blue, Edward looks up Gdansk on Wikipedia, and goes on from there. Gdansk is where something called the Solidarity Movement was born. This requires a word journey through the internet by Edward, who has a tendency to drift away in class when matters that have no relevance to the present or future lives of anybody at all are being explained: he does a lot of drifting. He's not completely sure about the meaning of words like *strike*, *communism* and even of *solidarity* itself, since they've never been uttered in his presence, and he has no idea at all about other words such as *foreign credit*, *trade union* or *Warsaw Pact*, which as far as Edward is concerned might have been Polish.

Seeking to work out what the word 'home' might actually mean for Mr Sienkiewicz, Edward looks at photographs of Gdansk, which was called Danzig in German. As he looks through the photos he quietly sings to himself '*Baby, I'm Danzig in the dark, with you between my arms,*' *t*o the tune of Ed Sheeran's *Perfect*, wondering as he does so why nobody calls him Ed. Gdansk is where some of the novels of Gunter Grass are set: Edward tried to read *The Tin Drum*, which was one of the ones his Dad left behind, but has decided to put it aside until he's about seventeen. *Dom* is the Polish for home, he learns from Google Translate: 'dom,' Edward mutters, wondering whether that was what ET uttered in the Polish version of the film he remembers watching with both his parents, before his Dad.

Then Edward is surprised to see Mr Sienkiewicz looking back at him from a grainy YouTube video made in the Gdansk shipyard. In the video, Mr Sienkiewicz has less blotchiness on his skin, and he has blowy blonde hair, and he's wearing a very smart white shirt with a grey stripe running around the collar's edge. 'I look at it this way,' the man says, translated by the presenter. 'In the history of Poland since the war, there hasn't been an event like this.' It's definitely Mr Sienkiewicz: though he can't hear the voice because of the voiceover, you can always tell from the eyes. Hearing him speak properly like this makes Edward feel funny inside, as does the notion that Mr Sienkiewicz, whose words are full of hope, does not know what will happen to him. He has a square but kindly face, a half-smile on his features as he speaks.

'Whenever we stand outside the gates of the shipyard, we feel threatened,' Mr Sienkiewicz says.' But here, in this little piece of free Poland we have here, I feel quite safe. No one is telling me how I should speak, or what I should do.' He's a big man, but there is a playfulness about him that Edward warms to, and which he can still see in the old Mr Sienkiewicz. *Something suka*, he'd said about the woman, and smiled: *suka*, Google Translate says, means bitch, so it was pretty obvious what the other word meant. *No one is telling me how I should speak, or what I should do*: later, Edward will write the phrase down in his *Words and Other Things to Remember*, his personal book. Perhaps that's what Mr Sienkiewicz had been telling the bearded policeman after all: perhaps it was his memory of the sensation of the gloved hands of policemen on his arm that had made him so angry.

The safe place the man is describing is what he feels to be his true home, the Lenin Shipyard in Gdansk where, following the sacking of Anna Walentynowicz, the workers refused to work, and from their refusal to work the Solidarity Movement arose. After much suffering, ten years later, their leader, a man called Lech Walesa with a brilliant moustache, came to power, and they'd triumphed over their oppressors. Edward has not before heard of such things happening in the real world, and certainly not to anyone he's met and spoken to himself, not unless you counted Mohammed Gailen letting down the tyres on Mr Cowans' Renault Twingo after failing history.

Mental arithmetic is not Edward's strong point, so it takes more than three minutes and a sheet of paper that looks like Einstein's blackboard before he's able to work out that Mr Sienkiewicz was born in 1945: he's frankly no good at guessing adults' ages, but yes, the man in the video looked about right for 1980. *Gdansk 1945*, he types into YouTube, and up comes a video of a city in ruins, bombed by the Nazis who killed so many millions of Mr Sienkiewicz's fellow Poles, and who would perhaps have killed Mr Sienkiewicz himself had he not had the good fortune to survive being born into a city in ruins, about to be conquered by the Soviet Army who would then wreak their own havoc upon it. Is it any wonder, thirty-five years later, in a shipyard in Gdansk, that you'd want to stand up and fight? If Mr Sienkiewicz was now rough-faced and large and smelt bad, it was because he was stuffed so full of history. How could a man and his farts ever smell good, when his life was stuffed so full of the evils that had been done to him and to his people and to their city, their country? How had Mr Sienkiewicz found it inside him to become a hero after all that? Why was nobody telling Edward about all of this? *I feel quite safe*, Mr Sienkiewicz had said. For some people, Edward can see, that in itself is a victory.

In 1970 shipyard workers were killed by the communist authorities in Gdansk. There's a monument to them at the entrance to the shipyard, on which appear the words:

Który skrzywdziłeś człowieka prostego
Śmiechem nad krzywdą jego wybuchając

'*You who wronged a simple man/ Bursting into laughter at the crime...*' Edward reads. He notes it down in his *Book of Words and Other Things to Remember*, and then below it effortfully transcribes the words in Polish, muttering to himself the strange and beautiful words as he thinks they might be pronounced. He continues his internet search, understanding what he can, knowing that he won't be able to leave this alone. If Mrs Starling, his history teacher, were to give him a quiz about the Solidarity Movement, then he'd probably fail it: there are too many people, too many dates, too many ideas, too many new words to take it all in. But Edward knows that he's learned the essential thing: in 1980 Mr Sienkiewicz finally reached a place of safety, but has now lost it again. Who could ever be angry if you offered a man like that your home?

It is 11:47 at night. His mum and Craig have fallen asleep on the sofa while on the telly Nigel Farage, who hasn't noticed that here in Rainow Road nobody is listening, continues to spout out stuff in that pompous voice of his; his mum had called Edward down to ask if he wanted to watch, feeling as she did that they should spend more time together watching rubbish as a family, but tonight Edward had more important issues to attend to. Now he goes downstairs and quietly lets himself out, unlocks his Raleigh and cycles the mile or so along damp, weakly-illuminated roads, first to St Peter's whose doors are locked, and then to the tunnel by the railway station. There are two people asleep down there in the dankness, and from a safe distance Edward shines his torch on them, making them grunt and turn over. One of them tells Edward to piss off: but neither of them is Mr Sienkiewicz.

Two months pass by without Edward seeing Mr Sienkiewicz. He doesn't reappear in the park: someone his mum knows who works at the hospital says she thinks she saw him being brought in after a stroke. 'Was he all right afterwards?' asks Edward. His mum says she doesn't know, that she didn't think to ask, and Edward wonders what kind of person his mum must be, not to wonder about something like that. 'I was in a rush,' she explains. 'I'm not a monster, Edward. I'm just always in a rush.'

It's when Edward is pulling his bedroom curtains to one evening that he looks down into the street to see Mr Sienkiewicz fatly standing there, or rather leaning against a lamppost, head bowed just as he'd imagined him after the policeman walked him away. There's a kind of continuity to that which to Edward feels right and lovely. His mum and Craig are asleep in front of the television. Edward runs out into the street in his pyjamas and tells Mr Sienkiewicz to wait until everyone's gone to bed, but Mr Sienkiewicz doesn't really seem to understand him: it's as though he's used up all of his remaining powers in just getting as far as the lamp post outside 37 Rainow Road.

One hour later, about half of which is taken up with getting Mr Sienkiewicz up off the pavement where he'd decided to lie down, then through the front door and up the stairs, all without waking up his mum and Craig, Mr Sienkiewicz is lying on Edward's bed with his socks and shoes off: the window has had to be opened. It's clear that he does, in fact, need new socks. So far he hasn't said anything except, at one moment on the stairs, the word *Edzio*. He's giving no sign of knowing where he is at all, but, Edward supposes, the important thing is that he got there. Wherever he's come from, it must have taken him all day.

'You've not brought your bottle with you,' Edward whispers, 'that's good.' Mr Sienkiewicz's ankles are big and puffy, and all sorts of funny colours, colours nobody's ankle should ever be.

'I saw you in a video,' he says. 'You were wearing a shirt with a grey stripe on the collar. Do you remember, Mr Sienkiewicz? The shipyard in Gdansk?'

Mr Sienkiewicz half-opens his eyes and turns to look at Edward, who has turned his desk chair round to face him. 'Gdansk,' Mr Sienkiewicz says, and then turns away and closes his eyes again.

'That's right, Mr Sienkiewicz. It was a great time, that was. June 1980. All of you locked in there together in the shipyard, behind the fences. People coming from far and wide bringing you stuff, food, blankets. Doctors came to look after you, and priests as well. Not only from Gdansk but from other countries, too. From all over, they came. Do you remember, Mr Sienkiewicz? Nearly forty years ago, it was. My mum wasn't even born. Do you remember all that?'

Mr Sienkiewicz's fat chest slowly rises and falls, and he makes a small gurgling noise which might mean that he remembers, but also that he might not.

'On August 31st,' Edward goes on, 'Poland was allowed to have trade unions. You were free at last to say and think what you wanted, Mr Sienkiewicz. No one was telling you how you should speak, or what you should do. And what you said about the shipyard being a safe place, well it wasn't just the shipyard any more.' He has to work to keep his voice down: it won't do to have his mum come in at 12:30 am to find him talking about the end of Communism to that paedophile from the park he wasn't supposed to be talking to. 'It wasn't just Gdansk. It was the whole of Poland. East Germany, Czechoslovakia, Hungary, Romania, other places too. It's fantastic what you did there, Mr Sienkiewicz, when you think about it. You helped to make a proper home for everyone. We all have equal stomachs, is what you all told each other. I've thought about it. If you don't mind me saying so, Mr Sienkiewicz, you're actually a bit of a hero.'

Over the past two months, during his wait for Mr Sienkiewicz's homecoming, Edward has gone often through this scene in his mind: once he even dreamed it. In the dream version, a single tear appears in the corner of Mr Sienkiewicz's right eye and makes its way down his blotchy cheek, tracing a route through the bristles, before dislodging and plopping softly onto the pillow. But no such tear appears now, and indeed Mr Sienkiewicz is giving every sign of having fallen asleep mid-conversation again. Edward hopes that he doesn't relax so much that he delivers one of his farts: if he does that, it'll disturb not only his mum and Craig, but the whole of Rainow Road and environs.

'Hold it in the best you can, please, Mr Sienkiewicz,' he whispers. 'And it doesn't matter if it wasn't you on the video. It might be somebody else. It would be nice if it was you, but it's OK if it wasn't.' He pauses and sniffs, secretly knowing that actually, it really is the same man: it cannot *not* be the same man. 'Do you remember the monument at least?' he asks Mr Sienkiewicz. 'The monument that went up near the entrance to the shipyard?' He pauses for a second to collect his thoughts and recites the words: *You who wronged a simple man/Bursting into laughter at the crime… Który skrzywdziłeś człowieka prostego/Śmiechem nad krzywdą jego wybuchając…* It's great stuff, that is, Mr Sienkiewicz. Czesław Miłosz wrote it.' He'd practised the pronunciation on Ms Kempinski at Moat Hill during her lunch break: when she asked him why, he just told her he'd decided to learn Polish, and left it at that. Later it occurred to Edward that Ms Kempinski might have thought he had a crush on her, which he 100 per cent did not.

As Edward is reflecting that probably he does in fact have a crush on Ms Kempinski, he hears Mr Sienkiewicz mumbling in his rough voice, talking in his sleep perhaps. '*NIE BĄDŹ BEZPIECZNY*'. Edward is sure he's continuing the poem: feeling it would be right at this point to do so, he trundles his desk chair over to the bedside and takes Mr Sienkiewicz's right hand, pressing it between his own. '*Poeta pamięta.*' The words come very slowly, as though Mr Sienkiewicz is struggling to remember them or because he's struggling to find the breath, but the good part is that Edward can understand what he's saying, and that he's saying the words he should be saying.

'Do not feel safe,' Edward encourages him, urgently whispering. 'The poet remembers. Go on, Mr Sienkiewicz. Don't stop.'

'Możesz go zabić – narodzi się nowy,' Mr Sienkiewicz says, so quietly as to be almost inaudible. Bubbles of spit gather at the corners of his mouth. 'Spisane będą czyny i rozmowy. Oh,' he says then, drawing out the sound.

'You can kill one, but another is born,' Edward says. 'The words are written down, the deed, the date. It's great stuff, that is. It was you, wasn't it? Dom, Mr Sienkiewicz. Dom. I understand you.'

After nearly a minute Mr Sienkiewicz too says dom, twice, and then he sighs and falls silent again. He is tired: there's not a lot keeping him going now. He's had a very long journey indeed.

'Goodnight, Mr Sienkiewicz,' Edward says, when it's clear that Mr Sienkiewicz won't be saying any more words, at least not for tonight. He lifts a corner of the bedsheet and dabs at Mr Sienkiewicz's mouth. 'It's great that it was you. Sleep well.'

He pulls a blanket from the cupboard and, quietly closing the door behind him, makes his way along the landing past his mum and Craig's bedroom. There'll be hell to pay in the morning, especially if Mr Sienkiewicz takes the decision to go to the toilet in his bed or indeed to die in it, but what can you do.

Edward brushes his teeth for not as long as his mum always tells him to and then pads down the stairs to the living room, where he lies down on the sofa, kicks the cushions onto the floor, makes himself comfortable with the blanket and closes his eyes. Upstairs Mr Sienkiewicz is sleeping, perhaps forever, and if not forever then at least until tomorrow, when the sun will rise over Poland also.

A Haunting

A. B. G. MURRAY

Every morning, the ghosts of Sheffield's trees flicker on like faulty street lamps. They kept on growing after they were cut; up and up and up.

It's hard to get used to a haunting. Teenagers dare each other to slap the stumps like they're electrified. Birds plummet through the translucent twigs in dismay. But the thing with ghosts is: they want something and if you don't get it, they start demanding. So, the trees tap on shop windows and trip up cars and thwack the bums of passing builders.

The Council called in priests to chop them down again, this time with words. From the prow of open-top buses they glided in like a triumphant football team, gesticulating at where the trees' ears might be. Cassocks plastered to bellies, the priests ended their parade with clumsy karate chops aimed at passing pataphysical branches; still, the trees flickered up like so many middle fingers.

Next came the contractors who'd done the chopping. They doffed their hard hearts – I mean hats – but the trees burned even brighter. Councillors appeared bearing thin wreaths and thick plaques; the wraiths roared over their lowered heads. Exasperated, they ascended the stumps like podiums. The torches softened; their stand-ins stiffened into statues.

The ghosts had got what they wanted.

Six months later, Sheffield has never been so happy. Instead of polling days, we have pollarding weeks; whenever councillors grow too dangerous, threatening to undermine homes and lives, we simply replace them with a newer crop.

But Have You Seen it In the Snow?

TABITHA BAST

The worst thing about Christmas was that my brother came home.

'This is not for discussion,' Mum said. She didn't fight to win but hers was the final word. We made her pay anyway, every year. We gave her different silences, mine from my room, on my bed with my Walkman on, making her yell three times before I came for tea. My Dad took his elsewhere, his tread in the hall heavier in December, back from the Social late and to the point. Once school broke up he'd take me too, sometimes. He played pool with the other men and made his pints last. I watched and ate salt and vinegar crisps.

The Social's too big for the people in it, and the walls are covered in photos of nearly famous Yorkshire people to fill the empty space. And there's a plaque up for the kids who died in another village scavenging coal for their families. It is bronze and polished, the only thing never allowed to get dusty. But it's up by the toilets which I don't feel is the most respectful place.

'She's a good one,' he would say to them, nodding proudly at me each time, like the men hadn't known me forever.

It wasn't up for discussion but it was Mum herself who raised it. It happened on the Sunday before Christmas when my Gran was over for tea. We'd turned the telly off because my Gran liked us to chat 'like a family', as if she didn't know what a family was.

There was cake; we were at the table in the kitchen, and the tablecloth was on.

'Move your feet,' Mum nagged Dad, to show she loved him. He pounded both soles down hard on the linoleum. To show he didn't care.

'God's sake, Jim, he's family, he's our son, and he only comes back once a year… and it's Christmas.' She faltered and it was only the second time ever I'd seen her nearly cry. Although my Gran says when the strike broke Mum was red eyed afterward for a year, like nothing would be all right again.

We went a bit sheepish then. And my Gran – bit rich coming from her who won't ever come over for tea when he's here – frowned at us over her reading glasses and started talking loudly about something she half remembered from the radio, that I half remembered her telling us before.

Mark drove up from London on Christmas Eve, later in hours every year. Now he arrives in the dark, stealthy and secret as if the village won't notice. He parks his car outside our house though, bold as brass, and if my Mum and Dad weren't who they were it would have got keyed each time. Or more. Traditions are built like this.

Me and Dad were out at the Social when Mark arrived. This time it was packed and full of ancient tinsel sellotaped to its square magnolia walls, smelling of fresh wet dog. It was the only pub left in town so there wasn't exactly anywhere else for the men and kids to go to get away from the frantic last minute cooking and wrapping, and it was pissing down outside.

I hung out with some other girls from my class and we talked about boys and music and I pretended to know more of both than I did. The Dads were pretending too, looking away when we sipped their beers. Mostly it was men and kids, but there was also a table of widows in the corner, being the loudest drunks of all.

'Will I buy her a cider, Jim?' My Dad's friend said, shooting a pound out his pocket like a magic trick. I perked up and my Dad shrugged. The girls looked envious. He got me half a cider and set it down carefully on the round brown table in front of me, with a Foster's coaster stuck to the glass bottom and a wink.

'There you go, love. Start young, nowt else to do but drink round here. It's good your Dad has you. At least.'

My Dad went rigid and silent which is something to be afraid of. It isn't just me who knows that, and everyone went a bit quiet except the drunk, deaf widows. He bent down slowly and pocketed the black ball in one. Then placed the cue on the table as if putting his fork on a licked-clean plate. He swallowed down the rest of his pint in one gulp.

'I'm taking you home.' He says to me, as if it were me that mentioned Mark. I knew not to give out like I give to my Mum though. We were wrapped up and heading out when the door opens and in burst the Warringtons. They're all covered in white, not water, and the eldest one, from in Mark's school year way before me, shouts 'Happy Christmas! It's snowing!' And nearly falls over because he's half cut.

The pub cheers and I cheer too and imagine if I had a brother like that all handsome and happy and here.

I'm sad we're not staying some more but once we get outside it's just me and Dad and the snow and I'm glad. I say I'm cold and he puts his arm around me to keep me upright in my inappropriate slippery shoes. The snow is coming down fast and hard, already on the tops it looks lethal and good for sledging, if I'm not a bit old for all that.

He's chatting to show he's not cross with me. 'There is Venus. You can just make her out, but it's hard, in this.' He brushes the snow away from his eyes while we rush along, me skiing in my plastic flats, looking at the sky to please him although it's the worst night this week for him to point out stars I already know.

Mark's car is outside when we arrive. A red mini, cleaned up for Christmas, a hat of snow on its roof. It looks like Santa come early.

'Well.' Dad says, stiff again like in the pub. 'Let's hope he's got us some good presents, eh?'

The door sticks a bit in the cold, but Dad boots it at the dodgy point and we're in. The kitchen smells good already and the fairy lights are bright like in the Social and the fire is warming up the lounge. But Mark is here, tucked in a corner of the kitchen with Mum solidly between him and the whole village.

'Let's raid your Mum's sherry,' Dad says, kicking his boots off on the mat, steering us both into the other room where the Christmas drinks are. He doesn't shut the door, doesn't go that far. He pours us three drinks and pokes the fire. Mark hovers in the doorway, like he's not welcome.

'Hi Dad.' He says. 'Hi small fry.' To me.

'Mark.' Dad replies. I don't turn for him.

Mum moves in, leading Mark by the hand and sitting him like royalty on the sofa. She reopens the sherry and gives him a glass too. His glass is chipped, so she turns it in her hand so he won't see the imperfection, like he's a guest. Then she stands in front of her only son, her face to the fire.

'It's snowing out.' She says, queen of the obvious. 'Lovely fire.'

'Good coal.' Says Dad and looks straight at Mark.

Mark swigs the sweet red liquor like it's lager. 'The people round here have memories like elephants.' I can't believe he's saying that, going into battle, against my Dad, against me, against us.

'That's long, is it?' Dad bites back.

'Jim.' That's the voice, that one, when you don't argue.

'I left something at the Social,' fibs Dad, and he's off out again, without me, not daring to slam the door.

'Pies!' Mum shrieks moving fast back to the kitchen, and we all sniff to smell if they are burning.

'Don't you get bored living here?' Mark says quietly, so she can't hear. I scan the drinks cupboard, there's a bit of Baileys, some gin down from yesterday, and some minty green one I can't pronounce. I'm allowed what I want on Christmas Eve and sherry is the best worst option. I pour it up to the top of the glass. Mine's not chipped. I'm feeling a bit drunk now like I'm wrapped in cotton wool. Some of the older kids say heroin feels like cotton wool, that everything is safe and soft again. There's a few at our school on that now.

'But have you seen it in the snow?' I finally say.

She's back with a plate out before he can answer. 'Mince pie?'

We take one each, they're just a bit overdone on the edges. Mum opens the curtains, to look out at the weather across the village. The back to backs are all lit up and the snow keeps coming. Relentless.

'Will he ever shut up about it?' Mark says, and that's the wrong thing to say.

'You crossed the line, Mark! You crossed the bloody line!'

'I *never* crossed a picket line.' He answers glibly. I'm so glad my Dad isn't here.

'There's more than one way to cross a picket line.

'Mum, I needed out of here, look at it – there's nothing, no jobs, no hope, there's nothing, and all that other stuff was years ago. She,' he points, dragging me into it, 'was just a toddler! Tell him to stop sulking and get over it.'

My Mum won't look at him, she is just looking at what's left of our village, it is white as a bride left alone at the altar.

'There's you men with your hurt feelings,' she says, 'and then there's dead children.' She pauses and stares out. 'And they are not at all the same.'

Her hand is on her belly, as if she is touching a memory.

We're so quiet now we can hear everyone at the Social singing, not the words or the tune but distantly as if it were a time ago rather than a couple of streets away. Mum is smiling, but her face is still sad.

'I'll wash up.' She's back to the kitchen, one room to another like she doesn't know where to be when he's here. Above the distant chorus I hear the tap running failing to get hot enough. I am eyeing my presents from Mark under the tree, three of them in gold paper. I want them, even though it's dirty money, with his job at the Met.

'Mum, I don't think I'll come back next year.' Mark calls through, his voice higher, like it's breaking all over again.

There's a pause before she replies, she stands there watching the soft fat snow laying itself like hope over our town, her hands in soap suds like a cheap imitation of it.

'Suit yourself.' She answers at last, intricate and cold as a snowflake.

I look out the window and wonder if it will settle.

Losing Control

MATT HILL

I cursed into my A to Z as the tube rattled into sunlight. A Central London police lockdown meant I'd missed my coach back to Bradford. Now I was forced to hitch home. I had to get to Scratchwood Services from Edgware Station, but it was off the map.

The station exit was choked with groups of rowdy teens. Probably just joshing about before a night out, but my guts tightened. I pocketed the map and strode past them, looking ahead as if I knew where I was going.

Away from the crowds a young man with spiky hair and a tweed jacket was locking up a library.

'Excuse me, can I walk to Scratchwood Services from here?'

He turned and narrowed his eyes. I took in his CND and, 'Nuclear power? No thanks!' lapel badges.

'Hitching, eh? Good fucking luck! Go left at the roundabout, right at the dual carriageway then left through the park. Ignore the winos, keep going under the railway and the M1, left on the road by the scrapyard and you'll be there. Simple.'

I tried to take in his instructions as he inspected me.

'Been on the march?'

'Yeah, police have blocked off the roads.'

'Fucking filth! What was it like? These bastards wouldn't give me the fucking day off.' He jerked his head at the library building as if his oppressors were still inside.

I tried to lighten his mood. 'It was cool, loads of people.'

'Perhaps the Tory bastards will see sense, but I fucking doubt it,' he said and turned away.

I left the foulmouthed librarian, anxious about the park drunks and not sure I could remember the way past them. The sky darkened as I wandered alongside the dual carriageway. The park trees further blotted the light. I heard murmuring, spotted the pitch-black arch under the motorway and ran for it. Heart pounding I emerged to deep barking behind corrugated iron and pushed on toward Scratchwood's tall lights.

The services were busy, plenty of people and coaches, but none was mine. On the slip road there were no other hitchers for competition. Shielded from darkness by the motorway lights I was feeling good. I stuck my thumb out, smiled and made eye contact with every driver leaving the services.

After five minutes two beautiful women in a Mini smiled and stopped about fifty yards past me. It felt too good to be true. I ran towards them and made it level with the car door before they sped off waving and laughing. No one stopped for the next hour. The whole sky inked black as I waited. A couple of drivers veered away as if I would leap into their moving cars. At last a sleek saloon pulled up, an electric window slid down, and the driver said,

'Where are you headed?'

'Bradford.'

'I can drop you on the M62. You should be able to get a lift to Bradford from there.'

'Great!' I said and opened the passenger door. Sliding onto the leather seat I was enveloped in acrid grey smoke. My hitch drew on a slim cigar, accelerated hard and grinned at me as I took in my surroundings. His shiny double-breasted jacket covered a pale blue t-shirt and gold flashed from his hands and neck. I tried to ignore this and played a complimentary opening.

'This is the plushest ride I've ever had.'

'BMW 735i with all the options. 155mph fuel injected leather and walnut clad top speed.'

'Cool,' I lied, 'are you going far?'

'Yep, back to Selby tonight. Two hours non-stop if you can keep me awake.'

You lose control when hitching. London to Selby takes three and a half hours at the speed limit. Flash Harry was probably going to cruise at around a hundred and was tired. My philosophy was that the chances of a crash during any hitch were slim; if they were alive to pick me up, they'd probably be alive to set me down.

'Sounds like a good deal, especially after the day I've had.'

'Tell me about it.'

That was the start of the contract. He gave me a lift and in return I would talk to him about whatever he wanted. I told him about missing the coach, the sweary librarian and getting spooked in the park. He smoked, smiled and kept the car in the fast lane, flashing anyone in his way from twenty feet behind. While I was speaking he leaned over and scrabbled in the glove compartment for a new cigar then lit it with the stub of the old. All accomplished while weaving just within the fast lane. I was transfixed and stopped talking. My hitch exhaled a lungful of wet smoke and stared back at me.

'Go on then. What was the march like?'

'There must have been a million there. I reckon we're going to stop it.'

'No chance!'

'What do you mean?'

'Right, so even if there were a million on the march that means there were 55 million who don't give a toss. Your march won't even skim my mates' consciousness. We're all living in our own little bubbles. I bet yours makes you feel as safe as mine makes me.'

'What do you mean?' I said, 'I get challenged at uni. I've changed loads because of it.'

'Ah,' he raised an eyebrow and smiled, 'but you're meeting tonnes of new people at uni. Loads of them very different from you. Where are you from?' he said.

'Great Yarmouth.'

'I knew it!' he blared the horn at a fast lane hogger who had forced him to drop to 80.

'You probably met your first northerners at Bradford, eh? First gays, lesbians, vegetarians, black people, Jewish people, Pakistani people? In the first couple of weeks you were bright-eyed and bushy-tailed, getting friendly with everyone you met. Then you started to select those to spend most time with, those you felt comfortable with. I think I must meet a dozen new people a year, tops, in my regular work and social life. Most of them are almost mirror images of me or the wife. That's why I pick up hitchers. I want to find out what you people think. I need to be challenged, shown alternatives to my point of view.'

'And to be kept awake!'

'Yeah, yeah; you got me there.' He nodded and smiled.

Hitching involves a power dynamic. You can be kicked out at any point; left on the hard shoulder miles from a junction with vehicles roaring past, or on the pitch-black verge of a deserted trunk road. In either case you're probably stuck for some time, so it generally pays to be pleasant and engaging. Sometimes though, you're picked up by someone desperate for an argument, someone who wants to test you. This guy had sought me out for a difference of opinion, so I was starting to feel I could open up. After a pause he resumed.

'So, come on then, educate me! If there's going to be a poll tax, why should I protest against it?'

He was driving so fast the motorway lights made his profile flicker.

'Because it's unfair! Everyone paying the same when some can afford more. Those that can't afford it are less likely to be Tories and won't register to vote. The bloody Tories are gerrymandering the whole bloody country! They're not moving the constituency boundaries; they're disenfranchising a whole section of society! They'll force out the poor and leave the electoral roll stuffed with Tory voters.'

My hitch took a long, slow pull on his cigar while he contemplated my outburst, then responded, locking eyes with me and only glancing at the road ahead when he took a breath.

'The American revolutionaries said, "No taxation without representation", but I reckon that cuts both ways. How about we have no representation without taxation? With just the same say as the poorest in how our taxes are spent, those who are richer deserve to pay the same taxes as poorer people. The rich don't use up more public money. They're probably using less by going to private schools and doctors. Why should they pay more?

'Because they can!'

'I guess from that you're not rich?'

'Yeah, so?'

'So, it's easy to ask for others to pay more, as long as you don't need to.' Cigar ash fell with the jab of his finger on 'you'.

'You're right, I don't have much personally at stake, but what about the weakest in society, who's going to speak up for them?'

'Ah, you're the knight on a white charger now? Have you asked them, the weakest, what they want?'

'They were out there with us today! Unemployed, kids, elderly.'

My hitch shook his head, 'Not the majority, I've already told you.'

'Because most are probably like my mum and dad. They can't afford to take time off working in the service sector. Jobs that are needed on a weekend.'

'OK, OK,' my hitch shook his head and smiled, 'so not all anti-poll taxers marched today.'

I waited in silence for the next round, pressed my right foot hard into the passenger footwell when a slower car drifted towards the fast lane. My hitch blasted the trespasser back to the middle lane with horn and full beam. He hadn't lifted a millimetre from the accelerator. Then he said,

'How were the police today?'

'They were mostly grim faced. A few had the carnival spirit, but I heard there was a bit of violence.'

'You heard?'

'Yeah, I was having coffee with a woman I met on the march while it happened.'

'Ah! The arousal of conflict.' My hitch leered over.

'It was only a coffee!'

'Did you get her number?'

'Yeah, she's called Marie, but she's at Warwick Uni, miles from Bradford.'

'Only an hour or so by car or hitching. That's a result! Kindred spirits meeting on a march, I bet the mood around you was good too.'

'Yeah, the best at any march I've been on. It felt like normal people were out against the system.'

'How did the police cope with the different type of marchers?'

'They didn't like our singing!'

'What singing?'

'The bonfire song, you know? It's to the tune of "Oh my darling Clementine"?'

'No, not heard it.'

'Build a bonfire, build a bonfire, put the Tories on the top, put the po-lice in the middle and burn the fucking lot!'

'Charming! I know the police pretty well. They're just normal people, trying to look after their families. Trying not to get murdered. You know about Keith Blakelock?'

'What, the Tottenham riots guy?'

'Yeah, he was killed by the mob when he was trying to protect firemen. That was less than five years ago. That imagery in your song, fire and death from mob violence, I bet that chills the bones of any copper, especially any that had been at Broadwater Farm. A mob of thousands, grinning and chanting murder in your face, no wonder they were grim faced.'

I tried to put myself in police boots; considered how we would have looked, outnumbering them, shouting, singing for their demise.

'You reckon they were scared of us?'

'They wouldn't know what might turn a crowd into a mob. Would you?'

'We were just people.'

Another pause. We slowed to the speed limit, and my hitch nodded to the police car parked up by the hard shoulder.

'There they are, keeping us safe.'

'How come you're such big mates with the filth then? Are you a copper?'

'I got to know them pretty well during the Miners' Strike.'

'The Miners' Strike? Were you a flying picket?'

He smiled over at me and his warm grey breath enveloped my face.

'Sorry to shatter your illusions. I was a scab.'

He searched for a reaction. I turned away.

'Traitor.'

'What did you say?'

I repeated the insult. My shoulder slammed into the seatbelt as we sliced across onto the hard shoulder and skidded to a halt. Almost before we had stopped he turned and laid into me.

'I wasn't the traitor! It was bloody Scargill! I could see we were a dying industry, any fool could. Government subsidy needed just to stay afloat, mines closing down everywhere. It was purely economic.

Then Thatcher turned it into class war, and Scargill led us out. He was proudly at the head of the miners, but he had no mandate. He never took a national ballot. It was undemocratic and bloody hard.'

Then he leaned across me and pushed the passenger door open. With his face so close to mine I felt flecks of spittle as he shouted,

'So, if you want to continue with the ignorant soundbites you can get out!'

Lights flashed and horns doppler-blared as lorries and cars sped past us anchored on the hard shoulder. I felt his rage and thought about getting out, but he was a real find. I'd been picked up by a piece of walking history. I'd seen and heard about the miners' strike when I was at school, but it had little impact in Yarmouth. When I got to uni though, my hitch was right, I had met my first northerners. Everyone who talked about the strike was full of the camaraderie it brought out in the strikers, and the hatred everyone had for the scabs. Here was a golden opportunity to find out about the strike from the other side.

I pulled the door shut and said, 'Sorry. I've been stupid. I don't want to get out. I want you to tell me about the strike. What do you mean it was hard?'

My hitch leant back into his seat and started to pull away.

'Now you listen up and don't forget this. I had a young family, new home, mortgage. Nice place. Mining was good money; hard work, but good money. Even before the strike I was worried about the future. I was casting about for a new opportunity that paid as much. My mortgage payments had been high, but they spiked during the strike. I couldn't afford to lose my wage, my family home, so I became a scab. There hadn't been a strike ballot, so I felt I was in the right. Others didn't see it that way. I got death threats, abuse, spat at in the street. The police protected me and my family.

'There was violence on both sides, but only from a minority. I had some good mates I gave money to when they were on their arses, striking. They didn't let on, the mob still thought I was a monster. I thought they were all idiots for following Scargill when there was no strike ballot, but I still felt their pain.

'So the strike ends, along the line we lose our jobs. We're all sitting on a bit of redundancy cash, looking for work we know, not just graft. We want something using our skills, keeping heavy machinery going. There's all this mothballed plant lying around. I got the lads together who I helped out in the strike. We chip in some cash to buy a lorry with a hoist and we're away! London will buy the plant, so we just scoop it up in Yorkshire, then take it down south. We start selling at auctions, then we get to know the buyers and it's mental! So much money for such little work.

'Five years on and I'm a director of my own company trading heavy machinery. I couldn't have done it without my mates. We stayed tight despite the strike. When it comes down to it, we're all after a good life, eh? Work and rewards.'

Suddenly my hitch swerved into a gap between cars in the slow lane. There was nothing ahead in the fast lane, no coppers around, just a lone smoker silhouetted on the bridge handrail as we glided by.

'Why did you do that?'

'Maybe it's superstitious, but I avoid people on motorway bridges.'

'Superstitious?'

'Yeah, from the strike. One scab was in a taxi to work, I bet he was starting to get stressed about facing the hell of the picket line. Anyway, he goes under this bridge and wham! Concrete block through the windscreen kills him instantly. Ever since then I can't drive under folk standing on motorway bridges. There's probably zero risk. It's half a decade ago now, but like I say, it's just superstition.'

'So, there's still an echo from what happened back then.'

'And there will be from what has gone on today. Maybe it'll stop the poll tax, but there has to be some way of paying for schools, roads, bins, libraries, and all the rest the council does.'

We lapsed into silence, so my hitch switched on the radio. We heard the poll tax march had become the poll tax riots. The will of hundreds of thousands of normal people obscured by a violent few. At the A1/M62 junction my hitch pulled over and turned to me.

'Sorry I lost my rag back there. I see red when outsiders dismiss what my family and I went through.'

He held out his hand and said, 'No hard feelings?'

I shook it. 'No, thanks for the lift.'

As my hitch's car blurred into the distance I thought about his legacy from the miners' strike. Despite success he was still haunted by the killing embodied by that figure on a motorway bridge. I caught myself contemplating the darkness beyond the lights. Then I felt the napkin in my pocket with Marie's number on it, smiled and stuck out my thumb.

Last of Them

AARON HAVILAND

The sound of the man's breathing forced her awake.

'God, you even look like her,' he whispered, leaning over her bed. His grey hair was almost blue in the dull moonlight that shone through the open window. He wore a faded brown suit, which was torn in several places and smelled faintly of damp.

It took several seconds before Clementine had realised he was there. Then, eyes widening, she clawed at her bedsheet and pulled it close around her body, suddenly aware of how naked she was.

'Who—'

The man placed a finger over his lips and shook his head. 'Let's not wake the house. I'd hate to make a scene. What's your name?'

She couldn't concentrate. She shuddered to think how long he had been standing there. The man pulled up a chair and sat beside her. His wandering eyes crawled like spiders along her skin.

'Clementine,' she said at last. 'What's yours?'

'George.'

Clementine noticed two men standing guard by the doorway, both of them over six-foot tall and built like stallions. They looked as though they had been in a fight, their suits ripped and patchy with mud.

'Don't mind them,' George said.

'But who are they? Who are *you?* I don't understand. You shouldn't be here.' The words poured from her mouth. 'Please, before my father hears.'

George put a finger to his lips once more. 'Everything will be explained to you in time, I promise. But not here.'

Clementine sunk back into her sheets. This was all a dream, she told herself. Just another nightmare – the same one she'd had many times before. The others didn't know where she was. How could they? They didn't even know she *existed*.

'How would you like to come with us?' George said.

'To where?'

He smiled. 'London. That's where they all are – not out here in the middle of nowhere. You ought to be with people like you. There will be plenty of boys to take your fancy. My grandson is about your age. He turns seventeen this month.' He paused, as if in a trance, and reached out to touch her auburn hair.

'Remarkable,' he muttered to himself.

As Clementine dodged out of the way, George seemed to snap back.

'Yes,' he said. 'Yes, I think you'll really like it there.'

London. How could she possibly go there after everything that had happened? She remembered very little – fleeting glimpses of yellow and orange against a cloudless night sky – but her father had told her the stories. Of the fires that raged through the city and the plague that had ripped through its heart. The rioting, the panic.

The *bodies*. In their thousands, her father had said. With too many to bury, they were left where they fell. They had only just made it out last time. 'I can't go back there. It's too dangerous.'

'You lost someone, didn't you?' the stranger said.

Clementine remained silent.

'A mother, I'm guessing. Or a sister.'

'Mother.'

'So you've seen it, then. You know what it does to the body.'

She covered her ears and tried her best to block him out as he described the event in detail. But it was no use.

'...so horrible,' he said. 'The way your fingers could simply – *push* – through the skin.' He motioned with his hands, as if forcing them through an invisible wall of butter. He must have seen the horror in Clementine's face because he looked suddenly embarrassed. 'Sorry. I see it so often in my dreams, I sometimes forget not everyone is used to hearing about it.'

'Please, sir,' Clementine said, eager to change the subject. 'This is my home – I can't leave. London is a ruin.'

'And who told you that?'

She hesitated.

'Father.'

'Then he's been lying to you,' George said. 'True, it's not what it once was. But then, everything must change if it is to survive. It must *adapt*. Don't you agree?'

'I suppose.'

There was a shuffle of feet at the door. Her father appeared, dressed in grey striped pyjamas and carrying a shotgun that looked almost as old as him. 'What the hell do you think you're doing?'

Clementine's heart sunk. 'Leave, daddy. Please, go back to bed.'

'Get the fuck out of my home!' he shouted.

George stood up from his chair. 'The girl's father, I presume.' He went to shake the old man's hand. 'My name is George. I work for... Well, it hardly matters now. As I am sure you're aware, we are—'

'It makes no difference who you are, so long as you leave and forget what you saw,' the old man said.

Though he tried hiding it, Clementine could tell George felt uneasy standing this end of a loaded gun. There was a slight nervousness to his words. 'It's more complicated than that. I have a sworn duty to uphold. For the continuation of the human race.' He pointed at Clementine, still tucked beneath her covers. 'Did you know you were committing a crime by keeping her?'

'Away from *your* lot,' her father added.

'*Ahh*. Yes. Perhaps you need reminding of the situation.'

The old man cocked his gun. 'I know as well as you. We all saw it. The world is already on its way to hell. No point dragging her down too.'

'I do not mean to *drag* her. I mean to make her a queen,' George said. 'How can you not see how important she is? She's the key to undoing all of this!' He stopped, as if expecting applause.

For a moment, it looked as though the old man had had a moment of doubt. He glanced nervously at the guards. The barrel of his shotgun dipped very slightly. 'Please,' he said. 'Please, don't take her. She doesn't need this. Just tell them you didn't find anything.'

'But we *did*, didn't we?'

The old man looked over to his daughter and she knew in an

instant. She wanted to go to him, to tell him to stop, to insist on going. Whatever they wanted with her, it wasn't worth his life.

The old man aimed his gun at George.

But the guards were faster. Within seconds, one of them had grabbed him from behind and hit him with the butt of their gun. Blood began to pour from his temple before he had even hit the ground.

The great hall was filled with near a hundred men of every age. Some looked as if they had just fought a war. Ties torn at the edges. Shirts stained with sweat. One man, sunburnt to the point of concern, had elected not to wear a shirt at all and was babbling nonsense about how this was all a waste of his time.

But there was one in particular Clementine had noticed – a boy, roughly the same age as she was. He had bright green eyes like emeralds and scruffy brown hair that, compared to the others', was only moderately greasy. He had been staring at her intently. But every time she caught him, his eyes darted away.

George sat quietly beside her. If he felt any remorse at all, he refused to let it show on his face. Clementine clenched her fists as hard as she could until they started to go numb. It was the only thing that would stop her from strangling him. She could do it. He had no guards to protect him now. It wouldn't take much to overpower him. The man was over seventy. She didn't care if they shot her for it. Then, at least, all of this would be over, and she would get to see her father again.

There was a dull pain in her chest as she pictured him lying there. They'd had to pull her from the body. The blood still lingered beneath her fingernails, no matter how hard she had scrubbed. Her clothes had been ruined too, though they had since found her something new to wear. A silk cream dress, as soft as moonlight. It wouldn't hurt to look pretty, George had told her.

The room fell silent as George stood up and made his way to the top of a high podium. He had swapped his brown suit for long, flowing black robes that made it appear as though he were floating. He took a seat in what looked like a small wooden throne.

'Thank you for coming,' he began. 'Today is rather special. After all, how often is it we come across something as unique as this?' He pointed to Clementine. 'Stand for us, my dear.'

Clementine rose to her feet, feeling every pair of eyes watching her like a thousand hungry vultures. The knot in her stomach tightened. She saw George mouth a few words of encouragement, as if she were a baby learning to walk.

'My name is Clementine,' she said, trying desperately to smooth over the cracks in her voice.

'Sweet girl. Frightened, no doubt, to be so far from your home,' George said. 'I am truly sorry for what happened to your father. It wasn't what I wanted.'

What did you expect to happen? Clementine wanted to say, but the words fell apart in her throat.

Then, as if reading her mind, the old man laughed. 'You must think we're monsters. And perhaps that isn't so far from the truth. But you're too young to know what it was really like in those first few days.' He let out a heavy sigh. 'It took my granddaughter. She couldn't have been much older than you when the virus claimed her. Heavens, you even look alike. I knew it the moment I saw you. It's the hair. Sweet as summer, she was. She deserved better.'

Clementine thought back to the night before. A shiver ran down her spine as she remembered the stranger's moonlit face standing like a statue above her bed. Was this some sick fantasy? To bring his granddaughter back from the dead?

'What was her name?' Clementine asked.

'Beth.' George smiled, and for once she believed it. 'Part of me still thinks she's alive somehow. I know it sounds crazy. I see her almost every night. But it's never more than a mirage. I see the torment in her face. I watch as the skin slowly melts away until she can no longer even manage to scream. Every night, it's the same.'

Clementine shut her eyes and thought of her home so many miles away.

'But losing someone close doesn't make me special,' he continued. 'I would bet every man here has lost someone. But the dreams of her, they aren't for nothing. They're a reminder. A reminder not to give up hope.'

As George said his final words, the room buzzed with excitement, a hundred voiced squabbling for their chance to speak. The debate had begun.

She needs a good husband! shouted one man.

Burn her, suggested another. It was the shirtless man, red-faced like a tomato, and almost as hairless. *She's obviously a witch. How else did she survive?*

The idea was so ridiculous. The knot in her stomach clenched so tight she thought she might collapse. Desperately, she looked up to George sitting atop his speaker's chair. What would Beth have thought? What would any of them? Why should they have a say at all?

Peering through the row of windows that dotted the upper balcony, Clementine watched as the day slowly faded into night. Hours went by. And still they talked.

I'll put a baby in her, sure enough, one man said.

But that was all she could handle.

Clementine jumped to her feet. 'Stop!' she shouted. 'Am I nothing to you? You act as if I can't understand! You've talked for *hours*, and in all that time you've treated me as nothing but cattle.'

George sat up in his chair. 'My dear, this is an important matter. It must be taken seriously.'

She wanted to explode. 'And *I* can't take this seriously? This is *my* own life! What makes a child more worthy to speak than me?' she said, pointing at the boy. Though, she quickly realised he had been one of the few not to speak. 'I think I would rather die than listen for one more second to you. So what if I'm the last woman alive? It wouldn't matter if there were ten. Humanity has lost. We've lost. And I would sooner put a bullet through my head than bring a child into this world.'

She had their attention then, and for a moment, she thought she had convinced them. A feeling of relief swept over her. There was an uneasy silence, as if no one knew quite what to say. She saw it in their faces. Then, a snigger. And another, and another, spreading like a virus until the entire room was consumed in mocking laughter. She could still hear the sounds echo in her mind, long after they put her away for the night.

The bedroom door locked from the outside. She knew there was no hope of escape. The white sheets on her bed made her think of home. Thoughts of her father drifted into her mind. She had managed to convince George and his guards to bury him in a patch of the garden where the poppies grew strongest. He would have liked it there.

Clementine opened the window as far as it would allow and looked out over the lifeless city skyline. What few dots of light that existed weren't enough to dull the brightness of the stars. The moon reflected in the Thames like a giant blue eye.

For the first time since they found her, Clementine felt helpless. Her only hope had been to persuade them to let her go. But they had only laughed. She walked over to her bed and buried herself in her sheets, not even bothering to undress.

She had barely managed more than an hour of sleep before she was woken suddenly by a sound outside her bedroom door. Keys jingled in the lock. Then, slowly, the door crept open.

'Hello?' Clementine said. 'George?'

'No,' the voice whispered. The figure stepped through the doorway into the moonlight. Clementine recognised him immediately.

'What are you doing here?' she said.

The boy's emerald eyes bounced between hers and the floor.

'Well,' she said. 'What do you want?'

He looked almost frightened of her. 'It was sad,' he said tentatively, 'what… what happened to your father. He must have been a good man to have kept you safe for so long.'

'He was.'

'And I'm sorry for how they treat you. My granddad wasn't always like this. He's not been the same since having to bury my sister. She was the world to him.'

'You mean,' Clementine said, 'you mean that man is your grandfather?'

The boy nodded. 'Ever since that day, he's been obsessed with finding some way to bring her back. He thinks he can undo all of this somehow. He won't accept that the world has ended. And I'm worried what he might do before that happens.'

Clementine wasn't sure what to say. Her mind was spinning. Had someone sent him as some kind of test? 'Tell me,' she said. 'Why bother even coming here? Why risk it? He'd probably have you killed just for talking to me.'

'I know, and I don't care. I want to help you escape,' he said, and handed her what looked to be a thick woollen coat. She noticed that he had one for himself as well.

'But–' She struggled to find the words. 'You don't even know me.'

The boy stared into her eyes, as if trying to study her soul. Then, he said, 'you really do look like her.'

Clementine gripped the fabric tightly and thought again of her father, all cold and alone. She nodded and slid the coat on.

The boy led the way along the corridor, through a labyrinth of rooms and stairs and out into the street. Broken vehicles marked their path. Hidden beneath their hoods, they made their way through the city, stopping every mile to check that no one had followed. After several hours, they reached what looked to be an old park.

'I'll have to leave you here,' he said. 'Keep off the main roads. Stay hidden, and you'll be fine. Travel only at night.'

He handed her a rucksack. Inside were various tins, bottled water and a blanket. There was enough food to last a week. Perhaps longer if she rationed.

'Thank you, Sam.'

Then, rather suddenly, he put his arms around her and left without another word.

The journey home was a long one. Luckily, the people living on the outskirts were sparse and paid her little attention. They had likely seen her as just another wanderer, cloaked in black to keep the midges from biting his neck.

When at last she saw the house, she nearly collapsed from exhaustion. But she knew she couldn't enter just yet. There were eyes everywhere, and they would have been expecting her to return.

So, she waited until nightfall. Then, as the sun dipped below the horizon, she climbed from her hiding spot in a nearby tree and walked the final steps up to the house.

It was empty inside. The air felt still, so quiet that Clementine could hear the beating of her heart. She found her old bedroom, with the window still wide open. Her father's shotgun lay on the floor where it had fallen. A patch of black marked the place where he had fallen beside it.

She gathered a few of her possessions and made her way outside. Her feet carried her to the far end of the garden where George and his men had buried her father. The rough mound of earth had already begun to sprout weeds, surrounded from every angle by dozens of yellow poppies. She knelt beside it and burst into tears.

'I'm sorry, daddy,' she said. 'I'm sorry, I'm sorry.'

Not far off, Clementine heard the sound of a car door closing, followed by a series of voices. She didn't have much time. She pulled the shotgun from her side and placed it beneath her chin. The voices grew nearer; they were shouting now, calling her name. But they had already begun to fade, drifting away into nothing.

'Clementine, don't!' George shouted. 'Clementine!'

But it was too late for her. Too late for everyone. The world had had its moment, she thought. It was time for it to end.

You will be free one day, my dearest India.

SARAH HUSSAIN

In 1896 the bubonic plague spread across Bombay and I had been working tirelessly to try to provide care for the afflicted. I myself contracted the disease and this made me feel weak, even hopeless, but I had to continue. I was not going to ignore the suffering of my people.

I know what they thought of me. I saw them sneering at me as though I was stupid for not making my marriage to a pro-British lawyer work. A man of stature, they thought; just because he was viewed in high regard by the East India Company, but I had no respect for him. He was an Anglophile; a traitor.

'Daama, a so called Philanthropist!' he would say, but it did not bother me. It was more the sarcasm in his tone, which hinted at a sense of misogyny that irritated me. It was like he knew I would be tainted by the divorce. Becoming a divorcee was like walking around with a sign on your head, which read 'whore'.

I was sent to England in 1902 to seek medical care. I woke up each morning in London to the singing of a chaffinch. This striking bird had welcomed me to a foreign land and woke me up just after sunrise every morning. I do not know if it was luck or perhaps a gift from God. I had been given a second chance. I was weak, but healed. I desperately wanted to return home, but I was there for a reason and it is almost like the bird reiterated this point.

And, that's where my story begins. It was a Thursday morning and I stood in Hyde Park, awaiting the infamous Kavana to begin his speech. He was not very popular for challenging the British economic policy in India, but after being married to a man who made excuses for the British invasion, I was honoured to listen to someone who was honest and fearless.

I looked down at the green grass beneath my feet.

'You prosper and grow, whilst my land cries,' I whispered.

'Resistance to aggression is not simply justified, it's imperative,' said Kavana boldly, as he stood upon the stage in front of hundreds of people. I had heard about his nationalist speeches, but when he opened his mouth, it was as though he was calling out to me.

As he came to the end of his speech, I caught his eye. I knew that meant I must wait to meet him. I felt tingling in my fingers and toes as I walked towards the stage and as people exited the park, I noticed Kavana talking to another Indian man. He had a long beard, looked serious – like someone important.

'Do you not fear for your life?' I said.

Kavana's eyes widened.

'I'm sorry, do I know you?'

'I apologise for my being forward, I am Daama... powerful words.' I squeezed his right hand as he held it out.

'Honoured to meet you young lady, please let me introduce you to the president of the British committee of the Indian National Congress, Mr. Naorobi.'

'It is a pleasure to meet you madam.'

It could not be a coincidence that I met these men. Mr. Naorobi offered me a job as his private secretary and I accepted.

My work began. Writing letters, filing important documents, as well as attending all his speeches. I learnt a lot from Mr. Naorobi, who insisted I was involved in all meetings. It was from these meetings, that we founded the Indian Home Rule Society, but for me this had consequences.

Dear Madam,
It has come to our attention that your participation in nationalist activities is a concern. Your actions are seen as a threat to Great Britain and we urge you to sign a statement declaring that you will

no longer participate in such activities, or else you will be prevented from returning to India.

The chaffinch continued with its melodic call outside my window every morning and I knew what that meant. I refused to cooperate. I would not be silenced and my work with Mr. Nairobi continued.

The next speech by Kavana was an important one. We gathered in Hyde Park, the sky grey, white flakes falling from the sky. The ice cold breeze whistling.

It seems the wind of this land is against us, I thought as the howling intensified, but fortunately, this did not stop the hundreds from gathering at the park. Banners raised high. A mixed crowd of both indigenous and migrant-folk stood together on the wet land, which was decorated with white flakes.

'Our voices will not be silenced,' he said. The crowd roared and the people came alive. Arms waving in the air, voices raised in agreement.

I felt a cramp in my stomach as it began churning. I made my way towards the stage. I needed to get to Kavana. But, it was too late. The shot sent the crowd into a frenzy.

How could a man with a revolver go unnoticed when security was surrounding the park?

He laid still, blood seeping from his body.

'You need to get to safety, Daama' said Kavana. 'Now…'

They had killed Mr. Nairobi.

The night was restless. I could not sleep. I saw the light outside the window, but there was no singing. I made my way to the window and slid it open.

The chaffinch was motionless on the ground. I hurried outside. I held the creature and kissed its forehead. I felt a cold breeze sweep by my face and in that moment I could not stop the tears from rolling down my cheeks. I buried the dead bird and then sat in silence alone, but my contemplation was interrupted by the sound of the telephone ringing. I went back inside.

'You do know it's no longer safe for you here, Daama?'

'Kavana, I have to carry on his work.'

'You need to leave the country, or else you will be next.'

I decided I would travel to Paris. Kavana had a friend who lived there and I hoped I could continue my work.

I soon learnt that the members of the movement for Indian sovereignty were living in exile in Paris and I was introduced to them by Rana, Kavana's close friend. He was also an activist; a man I could trust. We would meet up every week to discuss our next move. We called ourselves '*The Paris Indian Society*'.

'How can we get through to the people,' said Rana one night and then it occurred to me. 'Literature… we can educate folk by writing,' I said.

So, I began working on my first newsletter. This was going to be a piece that challenged the East India Company. It would tell the whole truth about the genocide and I hoped it would be revolutionary. The problem was I did not know how I was going to get the newsletters across to India. I continued writing and Rana made enquiries.

I began writing about ideology. The fact that British officials justified the invasion by stating it was a civilising mission infuriated me. I needed my people to know that the real reason they were there, was because they were looting the country.

'I have a friend who works for the French colony of Pondicherry and he has agreed to smuggle across the newsletters,' said Rana.

It was just the breakthrough I needed. The first piece was sent:

Our people have needlessly lost lives. The British have blood on their hands, I wrote.

I began to gain a female following initially, but soon gained support from further communities. I heard about an execution of an Indian activist back home, which only further motivated me, so I continued with my newsletters:

How do you allow the British to claim sovereignty in your country? They claim they are better and superior and yet they show us savage behaviour. Do not allow them to justify their claim to rule.

My words seemed to ignite a spark in many communities and the rebellion slowly began. Villages lost family and friends, as they defied their oppressors. But the sacrifice would pay off. I believed it would. I had to believe it would because I was the one who instigated the riots. I wanted change. I wanted an Independent India.

My published work had been noticed and I was invited to attend the second socialist congress at Stuttgart, Germany. This was another opportunity to tell the truth. I had to prepare, so I designed a flag. This would be a flag that celebrated Islam, Hinduism and Buddhism and it would show a united India. The colours of green, yellow and red, with images of the crescent and sun, along with eight lotuses.

The flag was ready.

On the 22nd August 1907, I stood up at the second socialist congress and said;

My people suffer due to devastating effects of famine. Enough is enough. We are equal and deserve to be an independent nation.

I then lifted the flag. There was silence at first, but then this was followed by a round of applause.

Perhaps, my words have been well received, I thought.

But, I was wrong. I returned to my temporary home in Paris, only to learn that Rana had been arrested.

'You need to come with us,' said a police officer as he pushed me against the wall and handcuffed me. I was sent to Vichy where I was incarcerated.

How could they do this to me?

I had been betrayed. France and Britain had become allies, which meant it was no longer safe for any member of *The Paris Indian Society*. I lay in the cold damp cell. My body ached and my brain felt defeated as it thumped vigorously, causing me a great deal of pain. But, I could not give up. How could I give up after coming so far? My health began to further deteriorate, so I sat and prayed. Prayer was my only hope. I could not die alone in a jail cell.

It seems my supplication was answered, as I was released and sent to Bordeaux, where I had to report weekly to the local police.

I then began to petition. I wrote to the British government:

I urge you to allow me to return back to India.

I really believed that I would receive good news. I waited and waited but received no response. However, after a few weeks, I received a letter. I stood staring at the words on the paper and my body began to shake. They were trying to punish me.

Dear Daama,

You will remain exiled in Europe. You are not permitted to

return to India, under any circumstances. If you attempt to leave the country, you will be imprisoned.

The letter flew out of my hand as I fell to the ground.

I was paralysed.

I lay motionless on the bed for the next month.

Would my pride lead to my death in a foreign land?

I could not allow my life to end far away from India. I know they were scared that my words were having an influence on the people, but this was all the more reason for me to return and show the people the importance of fighting back. I could not move my body, but my mind was still alive.

One night, I dreamt I was lying under the sun, the scent of fresh herbs in the air. It was almost like I could taste the spinach in my mouth. I thought I was home. But, I woke up and looked at the bare walls around me. I felt like I could not breathe.

I had to approach the government again, but it meant I had to agree that I would renounce seditionist activities. I knew that my literature had become widely available, so I worried little about agreeing to the requirements set by the British government.

This time, the response came more quickly,

Dear Daama,
Your request to return home has been granted.

They were just words on a piece of paper, but these were the words which granted me freedom. My life was in the hands of the colonisers. My journey to Egypt promoting suffrage had made sweat trickle down the foreheads of British officials. They had kept me away from my home for so long, afraid that I would ignite a feeling of courage within communities. I was promoting a united India, where people of all religions lived together peacefully, which, of course, would make it harder for them to divide and conquer. A woman from India, who had a voice, was a notion that made their bones weak. I was a problem that needed to be taken care of. So I wondered, had they shown me mercy? Or maybe, they knew that my death was imminent.

Their intentions did not matter much now. All that mattered was my return. My people needed me. They needed to understand that my sacrifice was essential as the conversation about gaining an independent nation had begun.

I returned to the blessed land in November 1935. I took off my shoes, as I stepped out on to the warm ground. The hot air hit my face and as I looked up, I noticed the colours, green, yellow and red in the far distance. It looked like a mirage, but as I stepped forward, the flag became visible and I said,

'You will be free one day, my dearest India.'

The Only Language She Didn't Understand

ROBERT KIBBLE

I can still see her eyes. So black. So deep.

The bouncer looks at me, seeing my short hair, my pale skin, my tailored suit, and he lets me in. I look the part. I don't feel the part, though. I have to stop shaking. I feel the phone in my left trouser pocket. I feel the phone in my outside jacket pocket. It's all set. Keep it together.

I'm in a packed hall. Hadn't expected there to be so many of them. People are talking to me, and I answer, trying to spout the rubbish I think they expect. I brush my hand casually over my smartwatch, starting my jacket phone recording. I glance down, even though I shouldn't, to check it's lined up. It is. I look away and try to calm down. Record and get out. That's all I need to do.

Such dark eyes. Such a wicked way of raising an eyebrow to make clear she was joking.

The crowd gets louder and restless, and then the speaker arrives. He looks like a bouncer too, with his oversized suit and his shaved head. He looks around the crowd, watching as the place quietens down.

'I'm glad to see so many good Englishmen and women in here today,' he begins, 'not like all the foreigners I had to get through to get here.'

There's clapping and whooping. I hate it. I want to run, but I can see her eyes, willing me to stay. I fight back a tear. Tears would be weakness to this lot.

'It's not like we're racist. But this country's full. I'm sickened to see you hardworking decent people, with your families, unable to get jobs, buy houses, alongside this swarm of scroungers who shouldn't even be here. They don't belong. They've got their ways, and that's fine, but they should have them in their own countries.' He looks around, smiling – almost friendly if you weren't hearing his words. 'They don't want to compromise with us, so why should we compromise with them? They want to change our way of life. Do you want to know what happened when I went about perfectly lawful campaigning in your town last month?'

There's a shout of 'tell us' which feels planned. Scripted maybe. Am I the only one without the script? I look round, turning a little so my pocket points around the crowd. I don't know which of them it was – I'm not even certain that they'll be here at all. Or indeed that I'll somehow know them. I need to capture as many faces as I can. I can go through the video later. When I get out of here.

'There I was, walking through a good English street distributing information, telling people the truth, a pile of leaflets in my hand, and one of their women – well, if I can call them women when they have to walk five steps behind…'

I remember her face, so beautiful, so perfect, framed by her dark hair. I can see it. I can see that black dress she wore to the party, the figure-hugging one. I couldn't help but put my arm round her waist, pulling her towards me. I told her how beautiful she was. She smiled and kissed me. I've never been happier. I don't think I'll ever feel that way again.

The voice continues, and I drag myself back to the room.

'…and hide their faces so they can claim benefits and no one can check. They're stealing from hardworking decent families. Like yours.'

She wore a headscarf when she went home. Her father was old, and she didn't want to have the argument with him. She'd told her mother. I'd met her mother. I liked her. Her mother always wore a headscarf when she visited. I remember her tears, the day after Sabi died. I remember how she reached out and held my hand as I cried. I wept in front of her. She stared at me, holding something in, maybe a lifetime of holding things in. A lifetime of hope for her daughter. Dashed on the street.

'…plus they all have a dozen children, just so they can get more benefits…'

We'd planned a family. We'd planned two weddings – one for each of our traditions – but she still had to speak to her father, and she hadn't wanted to yet. She was scared of that, which was all that held us back. We sat on a park bench by a children's playground and her eyes, looking at the children playing. She wanted children. She had so much love in her I wouldn't have been enough to love. We would have had beautiful children. Her looks. Her brain. Her wicked sense of humour. Even a small fragment of that would have made wondrous human beings.

'…until this one, she stood in my way and shouted, right in my face, that I was inciting hatred. Me! She tried to grab the leaflets off me, but I wasn't having that, so I pushed her…'

I look up. My eyes are pulled to him. Was it? The police said she had a leaflet in her hand when they found her. That's why I'm here.

'She got up and tried to hit me, stupid woman, and said something in that language they speak…'

English. That's what it was. Better than you speak it. And she could speak four more.

'You can't let them get away with that. It's our bloody country, not theirs. So I gave her a bit of a slap, the way the police used to do when I was a lad. When this country was great.'

A bit of a slap? I saw her, after. No, surely this can't be you. I thought it might be one of these hate-mongers, but the main man himself?

'She fell, and you know what? They're scared once you stand up to them. Once you stop the bloody political correctness brigade from interfering. They're bloody scared then. I ripped that stupid scarf off her.'

Oh God. It is him. I'm trying to breathe. Her headscarf had been ripped away.

'And then I carried on with my leaflets. As is my legal right.'

There's no air in here. My finger goes to my smartwatch. I press stop, and then start recording again, so the first video will save and upload. It has to upload. I've already sent my friends the link to where it'll be. Oh God, it's him. He's the one that pushed her to the ground, ripped off her scarf so hard it cut her neck, and then… well, she'd been repeatedly kicked.

'Now, if people ask what we're doing campaigning, we're trying to persuade our fellow countrymen to stand up to them. Make them clear they're not welcome. And if that takes boots – on the ground – well, all the better.' He laughs again.

I want to collapse. I want to cry. I want to get out of here.

I stop and start the video again, and then step back. One step, then another. Past an old man – maybe he's only hearing the fear, the hope that a country he misremembers somehow exists. Past a young woman, mouth hanging open, breathing in the hatred. Past a man in a suit, like mine. Well dressed. Businessman, probably.

I'm not far from the door. I could turn and run, but I know the bouncer's there, and I shouldn't draw any attention. I look at the time, setting up an 'I need to be out of here' kind of excuse. Turning, I take a single step and bump into someone. He's not a skinhead. He's well-dressed. He's got a face I recognise.

A column, in the local rag. Writes opinion pieces. What's he doing in a place like this?

'Wait a minute,' he says, and puts his hand on my shoulder. 'I recognise your face.'

Oh please, no. No. He did the report into her death. He came round. I showed him the picture of us in Malta, sitting in a café watching the world go by as we were stranded by that volcano. He was in my house.

'Sorry,' I say, 'I have to go.'

'Oi Baz!' he shouts. 'This one!'

The crowd goes quiet and looks round.

The door is ten feet away. A few steps, but the bouncer's blocking the exit. He's standing staring at me. Everyone's staring at me. I put my hand in my pocket and press the button on my other phone. The app I wrote kicks in. It's calling. I need time.

'I have to go,' I say, again.

'Not so fast.'

The large man from the stage – Baz – comes down and looks at me.

'What's this one then?'

'That raghead you hit,' says the journalist, lowering his voice a little. 'She was this bloke's girlfriend He's not one of us.'

So many men fancied her, and so many fell for those eyes. But the way we orbited each other's worlds for months before finally spending time together, the way she slowly opened up to me – me! – and the times we spent together, planning our lives, until one stupid bigoted man pushed her to the ground, kicked her, stamped on her head, and left her to bleed to death... left her to bleed to death in the gutter.

He's standing in front of me. He says something. I know now. It was him. I'm staring into the eyes of her killer. If I was stronger, and not surrounded by his followers...

One reaches forward and grabs the phone from my top pocket. 'He's been recording.'

I deny it, but I know from my voice they'll not believe me. One drops the phone and stamps on it. I hope the upload completed in time. Her face comes to me, and tells me to be strong. For her. I won't beg. I won't let them have that. My other phone is still working. I only need time. Time I now don't have.

'You killed Sabi,' I say, trying to stop my hands shaking. 'You killed the most beautiful woman who ever walked this planet. The kindest, the...' and my guts collapse as someone punches me.

I fall, and my eyes shut. I feel more kicks. I feel pain, but she comes to me again. She's holding my hand, and telling me to let the pain wash over me. She'll stay with me. I've done what I can.

Even though I can't see them I recognise their voices as they take turns giving their guilty pleas. The policewoman looking after me asks if I want to stay – she's noticed I'm shaking – but I have to. For Sabi. I still picture her face, more so since I lost my eyesight. I've been told I will walk again. They said I'm lucky to be alive.

As the sentences are read out, I don't feel what I was hoping to. I feel numb, with a grim sense of satisfaction. Of having completed a job.

I certainly don't feel lucky.

The Most Dangerous Woman
MARTIN NATHAN

Why are you so angry?

Today a white gate has appeared at the entrance to the shopping centre, with a sign above it saying 'random security checks'. The security guards watch people approach and then an arm comes out. The chosen one is directed through the gate. When it beeps you have to take off your belt, keys, money.

A man with dreads is shouting at the guards who look impassive, glad to have a job. He is angry at his selection. 'It's blatant... discrimination.' The guards don't speak. They don't explain. They just raise their arms each time he comes forward trying to avoid the gate. A policeman in a yellow jacket watches. A young black guy with hair bunched up in a top knot holds a yellow balloon to his lips and lets it deflate into his lungs, then breathes the nitrous oxide gas back into the balloon. He watches the argument and giggles. The man in dreads gets louder and sweat flicks from his chin as the security guards listen to his rant with the same fixed smile.

Glass fragments crunch under my feet, the smells of charred wood and burnt plastic sting my nostrils, as boys dodge past, whooping, their happy faces covered by scarves with slits for eyes, or hats pulled down low, beanies with holes poked out. Wild-eyed, they pick through shop-debris, yelling with triumph at anything they find... anything: there is a sudden trend for tweed, looted from Dunn and Co. the Gents' outfitter, now a burnt out mess.

The burnt wood still creaks. Sometimes the stack collapses a little further into itself and wisps of dust and ash emerge from it.

Deerstalkers are newly popular on the street. Everywhere young black Sherlocks investigate the damage done overnight and examine the evidence.

A young boy dances on a podium of crates, wearing a pair of old-man swimming trunks on his head, his locks poking through the leg-holes in heavy braids. He holds a handful of spoons and forks up high above his head, moving to a beat only he can hear.

A sour-faced woman, hair pulled tight, stuffs clothes in a suitcase, then tries to snatch the cutlery from him. He mocks her as he dodges each time. 'Coming for you… coming for you,' he sings, wiggling his hips.

A tall man in an orange T-shirt and Bermuda shorts lopes past, gathering empty bottles in a crate. Bottles and rags.

Shops have been torched, a settlement of grudges; other the shutters have caved in releasing the dreams they offer. The wig shop… people parade in shiny blue locks and sliver bobs. Now everyone is happy, sitting around talking amid the rubble. We're all friends, retelling and re-enacting favourite moments from the night… the throwing motions of lucky shots… the dodges evading capture. Everyone has a new swagger.

The tall Bermuda man wanders too cockily down the end of Atlantic Road, where the police intercept him. He feigns wounded innocence as they take the bottles, syphon hose and cloth strips from him.

Then the police beat their shields in a tribal rhythm, and advance down the road in formation towards us, and we stand together laughing defiantly until the moment comes for us to disperse.

'Why am I angry? Look at that fucker.' The man rested on his Sherpa van with its sticker on the back: 'No guns are kept in this van overnight' and he pointed across the road at the guy with dreads who danced by the reggae stall in the Granville Arcade, shirtless, shoeless, relentless in his dancing. The skin on his chest was tight and tanned dark, and his eyes closed, lost in the beat, in the rhythm of the sounds, the bass loud enough to pound a rhythm in your chest.

The man jumped in the van to park on the opposite side of the road, in front of the wig shop. Silver foil extensions hang from polystyrene heads. He adjusts the shutter mechanism at the fishmonger. 'Fucking stinks, that stuff.' He gestured to the tray of mackerel leaking icy blood onto the ground. 'Who buys it? Would you eat that shit?'

The stall holder grinned back at him.

'Every fucking day he's there. A fucking white guy and all,' he said.

White, but tanned dark brown because he danced from early morning until the evening when they slid the shutters down. Whatever the weather, shirtless, shoeless, dancing. He never stopped and he never spoke to anyone. Sometimes the woman on the fruit stall gave him a mango or a banana that she couldn't sell and he'd wave his thanks, still dancing as he ate it.

'It's a fucking disgrace.'

One day the dancing man was gone. No-one knew who he was, and why he danced every day for ten years and where or why he'd gone.

Everyone was talking about him now, asking questions.

'You want to know why I'm so angry?'

I was standing on Stockwell Road, where they'd kicked over the wall and stockpiled the bricks for ammunition when Zoe came out of the boarded-up cafe, with her friend.

'This is Brenda. She is the most dangerous woman in Britain.'

Brenda had thick glasses and straight cut hair. She nodded gravely and took out a copy of the Daily Mail, unfolding it to show herself in a big photograph on the front page. Above it the headline: *The Most Dangerous Woman in Britain*. 'It's not often the Daily Mail tells the truth.'

'In Britain? Do they include Northern Ireland?' I asked. The H block prisoners were on their phased hunger strike, the grim climax to their dirty protest.

She smiled. 'Yes. And I'm the angriest too.'

I realised who she reminded me of to look at: Ulrike Meinhof.

Brenda looked at me, sizing up whether I could be of use. 'I'm angry because no-one else is.'

★★★

Alan drops steaming lumps of pasta into bowls. 'It's spaghetti Bolognese. You do eat meat, don't you, if that's not too forward a question? The only saving grace of my cookery is its lack of ambition.'

A thick blanket of incense hangs in the room, masking any taste the food may have had. I look at the decorative junk all around us. 'There's a lot of… stuff here.'

He laughs. 'My housemate. If it's antique, he buys it. However gross.' He holds up a wooden tray of scalpels, forceps, clamps, gleaming in the light. 'It's an eye surgery kit. We can try it out later if you like. We've got glass eyes too, in case it goes wrong.'

He sighs. 'Sometimes I worry he takes his fantasies too far.'

Alan drops his spoon, close to tears. 'When he went to hospital he expected me to visit every day. Then he told me to stop coming. He said I depressed him. It's not my fault; hospitals are depressing places. Now he says we need modifications for when he comes back. I had to wait in for them to measure for a stair-lift. I'm twenty-six. A fucking stair-lift. He said I seemed angry. I'm sorry; the pasta is burnt at the bottom. Don't eat the burnt bits. I can't cook but I can make cocktails.'

He pours the remains of the pink concoction into my glass. 'Fuck the recipe,' he says and pours more vodka in.

The last rays of sun hit the field behind the house and the bare-chested man lies flat on the grass, twitching. 'He's always there,' Alan says. 'First, he likes to dance, then he lies down flat in the grass.'

'I'm telling you everything about my life here,' he says. 'I know my invitation was out of the blue, but sometimes you go with your instincts.'

He becomes thoughtful. 'Have you seen the store detective? The one who wears the brown leather jacket? What do you think of him?'

In Brixton the police are tall, so tall they stand above the crowd, able to see in all directions at once. The minimum height is six foot five. There is no maximum. They are recruited on the basis of their charm, determination and prophetic powers. They are always watching, high above the market crowd, signalling to each other silently.

'Go on Michael, tell her. He was there. He saw everything.'

I tell Brenda everything and she says. 'Are you sure that's what happened?'

'I'm just telling you what I remember. I'm not analysing.'

Brenda nods. 'The revolution only makes sense in retrospect. Trotsky said that.'

Brenda says, 'Don't ask why people are angry. Ask them why they're not burning up with rage… how they can stand it…'

She passes me the newspaper, and points.

'So you organised everything?'

'Single-handedly. The howl of English paranoia.'

I'm sorry,' Alan says, clearing the pasta bowls, with the remains of a watery Bolognese. 'That was horrible. I can't cook, but I can mix drinks.' He glugs more vodka into the pink concoction in a jug and stirs it.

I am there under false pretences as he lies back on his sofa in his purple kimono and blows smoke out into the room; the love chamber he calls it. 'We have a dungeon as well, but you don't want to go in there.' He smiles with forlorn hope. 'Or maybe you do.' He crosses his legs; they are shaved.

I go for a pee. The bathroom cabinet is full of pills and there's a cut-throat razor and a barber's strop hangs from a hook.

Alan is lighting candles and incense in the chamber of love when I return and as I put my hand down something makes me jump… a stuffed alligator that feels warm, alive… two feet long, jagged toothed, staring glassy-eyed.

Alan's voice is getting higher. 'I thought you'd done a runner. Last week I invited the store detective back for a drink. He refused to take his jacket off and left by nine.'

He laughs at the memory of it. There is some jazz playing.

'Fuck knows what it is. I don't buy the records round here,' he says.

He yawns, moves closer. 'They arrested him on Monday. They said his flat was like an Aladdin's cave, all he'd stolen. Five identical white guitars for the band he was going to start. Five black boys all dressed in white. Crazy… he spent all his day arresting shoplifters, then in the evening he helps himself building his dreamland. Such a fucking liar.'

I pick up an orange from the fruit bowl. I haven't had an orange for a long time. 'Is it okay?' I say.

He doesn't answer. He's holding a joint, glassy-eyed, mesmerised by the orange, and his head dropping towards my groin, dipping further, then he vomits in my lap.

'Stop apologising, for fuck's sake,' I say to him as I wipe the last traces of the Bolognese sauce from my crotch. 'Just stop talking.'

The night air is a relief.

Our landlord wore a fur coat, and as he stepped into the living room he put his hands deep in his pockets, trying to look optimistic. 'It'll be alright when it's cleaned up. It took six weeks to get the eviction order, and when we came they'd already gone.'

There was a mound of epoxy resin a foot high in the middle of the floor. 'It's going to take a bit of work. The neighbours said they spent their days sniffing and tattooing each other's faces.'

We could never shift that mound of glue. Sometimes I wondered what place that glue took them to, a place they couldn't return from even to find the toilet and so they chose to shit in the cupboard opposite. Week after week.

It feels good to be out in the street. No more of Alan's talking, walking at last in the cool night air, forgetting everything, except for the stains on my suit and the smell of vomit.

I feel my gums ache... and I realise I've gone too long without fruit. My gums ache and I head down Railton Road, past bomb-damaged houses, or buildings that have just collapsed from neglect, to the shop that never closes, selling salt cod and ling... all-night ackee, through a hole in the mesh and I'm running because the scurvy feels worse. My teeth will fall out if I don't get oranges fast.

The shop bell dings and the ghost of an old man travels behind the protective layer... between the shelves and the wire mesh armoured with Makrolon. He follows my finger, ignoring my words. 'Orange. Six.' Six fingers raised. He drops them in a bag. Takes my money. I ask for my change, but he's gone.

I pick up anarchist leaflets... activist events in Spiv's cafe. Refugee women: *Raising consciousness through constant revolution... Awareness through violent action... Preparing for armed struggle.* And a man with a mass of grey dreadlocks holds the wall for support, and watches me suspiciously as I eat an orange. He ignores me when I offer him one, and mutters contempt as I squirt the juice over my face, over my suit and fuck, I don't care… when your teeth are coming loose, you act fast, and the vitamin C is rushing through my body… to my gums. And I feel happy at last… I can head back to my flat, to take my suit off at last, to lie back on the mattress and eat the rest of the oranges.

Juice from the orange dribbles down my sleeve and a man appears out the passageway… rushing towards me, his hand stretched out… but I have no change and his eyes flick upwards and he collapses in front of me. When I roll him on his back, blood dribbles from his mouth.

'Frank,' screams a woman, and crouches next to him, looking at me for help. 'He's always doing this,' she says. 'Always.'

Frank gurgles up more blood.

The phone-box stinks of every human activity except prayer, but the phone still works, preserved for making important deals.

I look around to check for a street sign but the voice in the handset tells me where I am.

The woman stands besides and as I put the phone back she starts shouting, 'His kids, who's with his kids?' and then she runs off into the estate.

I go back to wait for the ambulance but Frank has gone, and I can't even find the puddle of blood.

A siren approaches in the distance with its flash of blue light.

I see myself from outside, as I tell a crazy rambling story involving oranges, blood, a suit stained with vomit.

The police in Brixton mean business. Operation Swamp. They don't like people who waste their time. Always know your enemy.

As the siren gets close I run off into the estate and I hide in the bin store.

We went away to Greece for a fortnight with the idea that fermented octopus and ouzo could heal the rifts in our relationship. My in-laws stayed in our Brixton flat.

When we returned my father-in-law had hacked the top off the epoxy mound and used it a foot rest or a place to rest his tea-cup.

He told us in the fortnight they had only left the flat for a morning trip to Marks and Spencer. He had stuck a map of the area onto a piece of card and marked all the murders that had taken place in the past fortnight. A red pin, except for pensioners, who had blue pins.

Murder Mile was the headline from the Daily Mail.

A serial killer was targeting old people which boosted the numbers. 'It's not that he's targeting old people that is worrying, it's that he's targeting the wrong ones,' my soon-to-be-ex wife said.

Either mentally deranged or very angry, the article said, lower down the page.

I get a letter telling me to go to the police station. The desk sergeant doesn't look happy and sends me to an interview room, where the policeman shouts. I should have been there last Friday. Why, what happened?

He grabs my collar and pulls me across the desk. Don't get lippy with me, son. He pulls me tighter so I fall across the desk, and I get the smell of his cigarettes and coffee blasting in my face. 'Do you want to know why I'm angry? Do you want to know why I'm so fucking angry?'

Then he lets go of my jacket. I straighten it. It's a new suit. He looks at his paperwork. Sorry, he says. I thought you were someone else.

I'm running, fast, really fast, and I can see the blue lights flashing on the block in front of me and I rush into the bin store, skidding into a crouch beside the giant galvanised bin with slop dripping into it from the chute and I'm gagging from the stink of vegetables rotted to putrid liquid, seeping into the concrete floor, mixing with pools of vinegary wine and beer. I tread on a carton that explodes, milk bursting out over the leg of my new suit and when I look down I see it's soya milk and I have to laugh because I'm under vegan attack, and on the wall there's a picture of a big hairy cock and underneath 'SUCK' in big letters with a redundant arrow pointing to it and 'Friday evening,' written underneath.

It is Friday evening.

The soya milk drips down my leg and the rubbish chute rattles as someone far above empties out more debris into it and fills the air with a new set of odours.

I start to get my breath back, trapped still by the police van and the ambulance outside, engines idling while they watch and wait. A couple of police get out and I stop breathing as they come towards me, but they carry on walking, and return a few minutes later with a stack of white packages.

I can hear them talking.

'There's no chilli sauce on it. I asked for chilli sauce.'

'There's some in the van.'

'It's not the same. Their sauce is the proper hot fucking sauce.'

They're taking their time. It's Friday. All is calm.

I'm not in a hurry. I can wait forever.

On the first night after clearing the shit out of the cupboards and hacking away at the dome of epoxy, we had some ether, from a little glass vial sealed with tape. I poured some into a bag and inhaled the fumes. The music grew louder… John Lee Hooker… his heavy foot stomping swelled until it filled the room and made the air shake. The first time you have ether it takes you to heaven on fluffy clouds, then it leaves you staring down into the abyss. You spin as you stare down, so deep in the hole, on the point of falling. The second time it takes you straight to hell. Every dream was drowning in shit in that cupboard.

Are you on some kind of medication?

'Do I seem angry? Of course I'm fucking angry. A fucking stair-lift.' Alan points, into the hallway where it will be installed.

I look up, impressed by the space around me, thinking about my flat with its dark corridors, the epoxy mound, and the constant thudding of bass beats from below. 'It's a nice house though.'

Alan grins. He leans over and I feel his breaths as he whispers in my ear, 'And one day it will be mine.'

When I took my daughter to register her birth there was an argument in the office. A woman was banging the counter in her frustration… they couldn't find her documents, and she was irate, spitting rage with her words. They buzzed for the security guard who came to help her to leave. The more he tried to persuade her to leave, the angrier she got. His calmness infuriated her. 'Lady, there's no place for you here, with your attitude.'

My daughter's eyes were just starting to focus. A tropical fish tank lit up a dark corner, and the guppies ganged up on an Angel fish, chasing it round the tank, darting to pick flesh fragments from the wound in its back. Then they fought each other for the meat held in their mouths.

We still had the lump of epoxy in the living room. It served as a shelf for the baby's bottle, for glasses of wine, for tired feet.

'Is that really what happened?' Brenda says. She seems angry. She stirs Fairtrade coffee with soya in a cracked mug, and it drips onto the floorboards. We sit on milk crates as she points to the map pinned to her wall.

I repeat my account of the events.

She marks with yellow dots the areas of interest, and with blue arrows the likely approach routes of the police. Red squares mark the positions she thinks we should take.

'Look… this is the point where it started. This was the flashpoint. That's what I said last week.'

She sticks on new shapes – silver stars, orange rings, blue question marks without explanation.

I raise my hand. 'I was at a meeting at the town hall the other day… there were some community representatives…'

She stops me and snarls. 'Community representatives? Who appointed them?'

Her face twists. 'I'll tell you what they are. Appeasers.' She spits the words with venom. 'They make me so angry. Appeasers and collaborators.'

When the police finished their food, they left.

I emerged from my hiding place into the street.

I saw a crowd down near the junction with Coldharbour Lane. When I looked down I saw Frank's pool of blood in the pavement.

A man was standing bare-chested in the street. I could see his silhouette against the flashing orange light outside the minicab office, his arms waving, hips swaying, rays of light heading towards me through the smoke.

A leaflet blew out from the stack at Spiv's Cafe: Chile – A lesson from history. I saw Brenda's picture on the back. The most dangerous woman in Britain.

Down the road there was an angry shout and a flash as a petrol bomb exploded. Even at that distance I could feel the heat on my face.

Suddenly the man in dreads becomes calm and compliant. The rage drops away and he heads towards the security gate. The security guards are watching him carefully, knowing this isn't going to be straightforward.

He stands in front of the gate, on the threshold of the magical kingdom, and he raises one arm and puts it through the gate. He lets it drop and raises the other. Then raises a leg, and puts that through. Then he begins to shuffle very, very slowly towards it.

The security guards mutter to each other, allowing traces of amusement of appear on their faces. One of them catches the policeman's eye. He is ready.

When the beeper sounds they are ready for action though.

The man shakes his dreads and steps away. The security guard points at the man's headphones and his belt.

The man with the balloon lets the gas escape from his lungs in a gasp, forgetting to recapture it.

The man in dreads is determined to get into that shopping centre. He takes the headphones off, hands them to the security guard. Then he takes his shirt off, hands that to him. He stands barechested, defiant as his locks fall down his back.

Then he takes his shoes off, unbuckles his belt and slides his trousers down. He stands there naked, gleaming in the sunshine and he raises his arms high and walks through the gate, triumphant.

Nachthexan

JIM LEWIS

1 7.05.43

Tanya is moving on the bunk below.

The searchlights pan along the sides of the hut, the glare leaks through the crevices.

The air raid sirens wail. All lamps in the camp are extinguished.

Now, in the dark, only the bitter east wind pierces the poorly fitting planks, sighing with its icy breath on my bare face. I shiver under my one blanket, although still fully clothed. The stove's fading embers give no warmth.

'Are you still awake Tanya?' I whisper.

'No,' comes her muffled reply. 'Katrina… Go to sleep.'

'I'm cold, can I come down? Two blankets are better than one. We could keep each other warm.'

'Big sister you snore and your breath smells of cabbage.'

There is silence for a while. Then Tanya relents, 'All right… and no talking.'

I nudge in beside Tanya and spread my blanket over both of us. Tanya too is wearing all her clothes and her head is wrapped in a scarf. The lice are moving and itching in my armpits and between my legs. I try not to fidget and scratch. Even through my padded jacket and Tanya's red army great coat, I feel her boniness. I had nursed her through dysentery. I made a point of saving the choicest piece of potato or cabbage from the watery soup.

There is the drone of approaching bombers, I judge it is from the direction of Dortmund, north of us. Sometimes they bomb

Cologne and they pass over us to turn away to the north and their home. But not tonight; the RAF are bombing Dortmund.

'Home…' I whisper. England for them, Ukraine for me.

I hear the distant thud of bombs and the sound of anti-aircraft fire. Even though they may kill me, it fills me with joy to think the Germans are getting something of their own medicine, here on their own soil.

'Give them hell… give them fucking hell.' Tanya chuckles, 'May they all burn in hell.'

Tanya hisses words.

'I hope they bomb and burn every Nazi to hell – even if I burn with them. They have it coming. I'll laugh as they weep. None of them is innocent. Bomb them and their children and their children's children – all the fuck to hell – comrades – fuck them to their deaths!'

Some of the other woman are whimpering.

The raid seems louder than other nights.

'They're growing in strength.' I whisper.

'They need to.'

The sounds fade.

'Now Katrina – shut the fuck up and go to sleep!'

I met Tanya for the first time in August. She had been captured near Nepokrytaia in May '42, in the fight around Kharkov. She had crash-landed in a lake, she told me. They carried no parachutes to save weight. Her navigator drowned.

'She was lucky.' Tanya laughed.

The guards called her Nachthexan – Night-Witch. That first time, I saw the proud defiance in her eyes. She described how, flying their old Polikarpovs, they were night stalkers. They'd cut their engine and glide over the German lines looking for the glow of cigarettes to aim their bombs on… men. There was only the sound of the wind as they glided in their old crop dusters.

'As if we flew on broomsticks,' she said.

'They feared us, so they'd fuck us, to diminish their fear.'

Tanya's blonde hair attracted the guards' attention. She said that this saved her. Any Russian woman in uniform was always raped and shot.

'They like their meat fresh when they can get it. But I've seen them fuck fresh corpses, staked over a gate.' She coughed, bringing up phlegm into her mouth, and rolled it into lump. Then she gobbed into the dust where a fly loitered.

'Fuck it! Missed!' She pushed back her fringe. 'My Goldilocks hair saved me!'

'We are things to them… men…' she says bitterly. 'They have no soul. But I am always a free witch… here…' She tapped the side of her head, laughing. 'In here…'

'Are you religious?' I'd asked

Tanya threw back her head and laughed.

'Am I fuck? You don't have to be religious to have a soul. I'm a good communist but don't let them know that or I'm screwed.'

Her voice was deep and husky from smoking, like that of an old woman, but she told me she was not yet twenty-three.

Tanya saw no problem in trading her services to the NCOs for cigarettes and food… to live. These men then gave her some protection from the brutalities of the others – the rank and file. This aura of protection extended by association to me. I'm often in her company as we exercise around the compound. At thirty-nine I'm less attractive than Tanya. I'm spared much of the attention the younger prisoners receive. After my capture at Dneprostro I find ways to make myself ugly – to be less woman. Before that day I felt I was a citizen – a person still – even under the terror, I was called 'Comrade Engineer'. I had a part in the building and then the destruction of our great dam, guiding the sappers to lay their charges in '41. But in Germany we are slaves. We are nothing.

I lay awake for a while. Sharing our body heats. The cold retreats a little. I drift off into sleepiness. I try to think of better times. I see the expanse of the Dnieper again shining in the spring light. The fresh green of the birch leaves are translucent against the sun. I am smart in a white coat reading the gauges and dials in the control room.

The aircraft engines throb near and low. Some have come back.

'Low – straining for height.' Tanya whispers. 'Heavy bombers.'

This time something is different. The anti-aircraft fire is rapid and close. Once – twice – the hut is shaken by explosion. For a moment – silence – then a third. There is a new wind straining through the planking. It smells of water and earth. I clutch onto Tanya, but she is laughing.

'Fuck them! Fuck them to hell!'

Some of the other woman are moaning and crying.

'Shut the fuck up!' Tanya yells.

Then she is swept from me. The world of prison dissolves around me.

The waters close over me.

I struggle…

I see my Dnieper, and it is swallowing me in homecoming.

I am home now. 'Tanya!' I call out. 'I am come back.'

But I gasp as I break surface. The Moon is full.

'Tanya!' I scream.

There is no answer.

I am rolled by the tide, clutching onto planking.

From the water, holding onto my debris, my body is cast ashore among corpses.

'Where is Nachthexan?' I say.

There is the sound of wind over the waters.

Nachthexan is free… she always was.

A State of Grace

BUD CRAIG

Where to begin? Election day 2113 could be a good starting point or maybe my thirty-fifth birthday on 3rd March 2114, when I moved back to the North East from London. But, no, the opening scene of this story takes place on a Monday in June 2118.

That morning I stood in front of the mirror in my bedroom, checking my clothes with almost obsessive care. It wasn't worth taking a chance. My black skirt was three centimetres below the knee, comfortably within the guidelines. It contrasted well with the loose, white jumper I'd bought the previous week. The high neck and long sleeves were as recommended in the most recent edition of the *Feminine Dress Code*.

I ran a brush through my hair, thinking of the words of the *FDC*: 'Hair must be long. God wants a woman to look like a woman'. I resisted the urge to liven up my make-up free face with scarlet lipstick, while wondering if God, should he actually exist, really had time for such trivia.

Going to the window, I looked across the road towards the first prayer group assembling on the far bank of the Loven. As they shuffled along in a ponderous line, their white robes fluttered in the light breeze. As the sun burnt down, they took up their positions at the edge of the river, a mere trickle since the drought started.

'Good morning, Henry,' I called to the heron standing motionless on the gravel in the middle of the river.

The MiM contingent pulled up in their camper van and began to unload their banners.

'Good morning, wankers,' I said, relieved that I would be gone before they started their chanting.

When I saw the yellow helicopter with the purple G.O.D. logo on its side circling the skies, I knew it was nearly time to go. Then my phone rang.

'Is that Julia Marston?' said a man's voice.

'Yes,' I replied, trying to place his accent.

'Hi, this is Hugh Franklin. I'm a journalist from Montreal. I'd like to do an interview if that's OK.'

'An interview?'

Questions ran through my mind. Did I have time? Would it mean more trouble? Whose side was he on?

'About SPOMM,' he added.

As if it would be about anything else.

I always walked the three miles to SPOMM's North East Regional HQ, following the valley, stopping occasionally to admire the Lovendale hills that surrounded me. The pleasure of the country walk disappeared once I arrived in Loventon High Street. The posters for the next public execution, red letters on a white background, screamed at me from walls and lampposts, offering 25% off if I booked in advance.

A crowd of MiM campaigners, placards held aloft, had gathered outside the *God's Own Finance* building on the corner of Sinless Street and Blessed Grove. When they saw me, the fanatics' voices got louder. The first cat call came from a middle-aged man, suited and booted, red hair with the regulation side parting. A chant from his companions followed each insult.

'Shameless Harlot!'

'MiM'

'Brazen Hussy!'

'MiM'

'Murdering Slag!'

'MiM'

Hussy, Harlot, Slag: such sweet, old-fashioned words. A woman of pensionable age lobbed half a brick in my direction. I ducked, hurrying past them to a cry of *The Sanctified One will be avenged*. Nobody knew who *The Sanctified One* was. Cynics suggested he was just a bogey man, invented to frighten us into behaving ourselves. Others thought he was the power behind the throne of the government, who made sure they kept on the right track. Or the wrong one.

As I walked on, I wondered what Ralph would say. *I told you so* perhaps. Had I done the right thing? I would have been safe with Ralph, but it wasn't about safety. The words of our last, pointless argument came back to me. Oh, Ralph, I said almost out loud. I hoped he was OK and wished he were with me. Too late now.

At the office two hours later I sat opposite a tall, slim man with untidy fair hair, wondering if I would ever practice sexual freedom again instead of just talking about it.

'So, Hugh, how come you've travelled all this way to talk to me?' I almost simpered.

From the moment he'd walked in the office, it was as though somebody had stuck a needle in my arm, injecting a large dose of adolescence.

'Well, your name's kind of interesting,' he smiled.

'What, Julia?'

Did that sound witty and self-deprecating or would he think I was an idiot? And why was I so keen to impress him?

'Yeah, but SPOMM is an interesting name too.'

I took a folder from my desk and handed it to him.

'Have an information pack,' I said.

'Thanks.'

He glanced at the words on the front cover for a moment before speaking again.

'Safe, legal, fun,' he read out. 'Neat slogan.'

'And true,' I said. 'Anyway, let's start the interview.'

'Sure. I guess I need some sort of background first. When I was coming through customs a big sign greeted me: *Welcome to the Holy United Kingdom. A State of Grace.* What's that about?'

'It's a play on words: The UK is a state, a state of grace is a condition of being free from sin.'

His frown suggested complete bafflement.

'So the UK is free from sin?'

'Who knows? Have you heard what's happening over here?'

'Yeah, but it's hard to figure for a Canadian, you know?'

'It's not easy to understand for a Brit,' I said. 'What do you want to know?'

He thought for a moment.

'Is it right that SPOMM was founded to, you know, get round the laws passed by your government?'

'That's pretty well it,' I agreed. 'In an ideal world SPOMM wouldn't be necessary.'

An ideal world, I thought. Not one run by God's Own Democracy.

'It certainly isn't necessary in Canada,' he said.

'Lucky old Canada.'

Trying not to stare at him – he really was gorgeous – I outlined the legislation the G.O.D. coalition had enacted.

'Wow,' he said, 'these restrictions must make life kind of difficult.'

'For most of us. The rich and powerful will go on as before.'

He looked pensive for a moment.

'Did people really vote for these guys?'

'Afraid so.'

His eyes opened wide.

'Well… why?'

I'd thought about it, discussed it and read books about it. Could it be explained?

'I can give you a few thoughts, that's all.'

Again that winning smile.

'I'm in your hands.'

I wish you were, I wanted to say.

'For years floods, power failures, water shortages, have all been getting worse. For most people each year was harder than the last. Nobody seemed able to make it any better.'

'Global warming, right?'

'Yes, but the people who are now in power put it all down to a punishment from God.'

'Punishment?'

'According to them, we have to get back on the true path. They said if we do the right things, God will solve our problems.'

'Right.'

'At the time of the last election I reckon the voters were getting desperate.'

'So they put religious fundamentalists in power?'

I nodded.

'If the G.O.D. guys were right,' said Hugh, 'there should be no more floods and stuff?'

I almost laughed, but it wasn't funny.

'That was the idea. There was only one thing wrong with this plan: it didn't work.'

He pursed his lips, screwing up his eyes in concentration.

'Did the government change its policies?'

I shook my head.

'No way. G.O.D.'s answer is to pray harder, place even more restrictions on people's behaviour and hope for the best.'

After the interview I decided to take the rest of the day off. I offered to show him round the local countryside, starting with Bentley in Lovendale, the village where I lived. Of course we ended up in bed together.

'Sorry about the bite marks on your chest,' I said, snuggling closer to him. 'I must have got carried away.'

He chuckled and ran his hands over my buttocks.

'I got a little carried away myself,' he said.

For the next two months, we got carried away whenever we could. My bedroom became a kind of cocoon, a defence from the real world outside. I almost forgot about the article Hugh had written about SPOMM. A Canadian magazine had accepted it but it would be months before it would be published.

One Sunday I walked to St Edmund's as usual. Regular church attendance had been essential since the decree defining atheists as terrorists. It also helped me keep up with the latest thinking. By then God's Own Democracy didn't know which way to jump. The opposition accused it of extremism; from its own ranks came demands for more oppression.

'My dear brethren, some people say we have gone too far,' said the Reverend Philip Kingston from the pulpit. 'But God says we haven't gone far enough.'

Philip, a plump balding Scotsman, hid the harshness of his message behind a thin layer of charm. This, coupled with a strong voice, made him an effective preacher.

'God willing – and I'm sure he is willing – there will be a law passed next week.'

He looked round the packed church – attendances had shot up since G.O.D. had come to power. His eyes rested at random on members of the congregation. The M¦M group were out in force. Today they looked pleased with themselves. Not a good sign.

'Yes, my dear brethren, soon all forms of sexual activity except those specifically focused on procreation and practised within the confines of holy matrimony will be against the law.'

Practised within the confines of holy matrimony, eh? And they say romance is dead. On my way out of the service I shook Philip's hand as he bade farewell to his parishioners.

'Ah, Julia,' he said with an avuncular beam, 'how lovely to see you. How are you?'

'Never better. And you?'

'Optimistic, Julia. Yes, I would say I'm optimistic.'

As I walked home, I pondered his words. The Rev Kingston was an influential man. He had to be taken seriously. If Philip were to be believed, it was no wonder M¦M members had smiles on their faces. God's Own Democracy was about to finish the job.

The following Saturday morning I went to answer the door of my riverside cottage.

'Ralph,' I said, staring in amazement. 'I thought you were in Belgium or somewhere.'

'Holland.'

He hadn't changed, but then what was I expecting? In his pin-striped suit, Ralph would always look like a lawyer. Rather belatedly, I invited him in. A few minutes later, we sat with cups of tea at my kitchen table.

'Are you back for good?' I asked.

He sipped his tea as though afraid it was too hot.

'Possibly. Early days yet.'

He seemed reluctant to say much. Maybe if I kept asking questions he might tell me something significant.

'Are you working?'

Another sip of tea.

'I'm, er… looking round, you know.'

For what, I wondered? He shrugged, taking the handle of his mug and twisting it round before speaking again.

'Are you, er, seeing anyone?'

Was that why he was here?

'Yes,' I replied. 'He's a journalist. Canadian.'

I told him a bit about Hugh, but stopped when I began to sound as though I were gloating. Then Ralph picked up a copy of the Lovendale Chronicle from the coffee table and glanced at the front page article.

'Looks like things are getting worse,' he said. 'This Kingston guy is getting a lot of coverage.'

'He has a lot of supporters.'

'The new legislation they rushed through. It could mean…'

Suddenly impatient, I cut in.

'I know what it *could* mean, but they'll never be able to enforce it.'

We sat in silence, not making eye contact.

'I'd better go,' he said eventually.

On his way to the door, he stopped, taking my hand.

'Just remember, I'll always do what I can to help you.'

'It must be great living here, Julia,' said Hugh.

It was a couple of days later and we were strolling hand in hand on the river bank opposite my house. Already a hint of North East England had crept into his Canadian accent.

'Yeah, it's been the same for years.'

As we walked on, I tried to see my surroundings through Hugh's eyes. I was determined to appreciate the beauty all around me instead of taking it for granted as I often did.

'It's so peaceful,' he said.

Just then, as though to prove him wrong, the noise started. We looked up. One of the G.O.D. helicopters was descending rapidly, the whir of the rotor blades deafening. As it dropped on the grass, I looked at Hugh. Unable to stand the din any longer I put my hands over my ears until the engine cut out. Now we heard only bird calls, distant traffic and the rippling of the river. I gripped Hugh's hand tighter.

Two tall, athletic looking figures got out of the chopper. The woman's long, dyed blonde hair, her tight-fitting yellow jumpsuit with its G.O.D. badge and perfect make-up didn't quite match up to the Feminine Dress Code. How did she get away with it?

The man's suit was similar to the one his female companion was wearing. He adopted a pose like an actor playing a conquering hero, his hair plastered down so that the wind had no impact on his side parting. They strode towards us.

'Julia Marston,' said the man.

'Yes.'

'I am Colonel Matthew Jones,' he said. 'This is Major Charlotte Flint.'

Hugh let go of my hand.

'What do you want?' I said.

'We have come to purge you of sin. Go with Major Flint.'

I weighed up the odds. She towered above me, exuding physical fitness. Not for the first time I wished I were a few inches taller and took more exercise. I wondered how to play it.

'Come on, Hugh, let's go home,' I said.

I looked to my right. About a metre away Hugh was standing up straight as though on a parade ground. A black Jaguar with tinted windows pulled up almost noiselessly by the side of the road. Hugh jogged over to it and got in the back. The car pulled away.

Grabbing my wrists, Charlotte took only seconds to drag me to the helicopter. I struggled but to no avail. As she flung me in and fastened my seat belt, I tried to work out what hurt the most: my wrists, the fear of what would happen to me or the overwhelming pain of betrayal.

Two days later Major Flint led me into a brightly lit, palatial room. At least it got me out of the gloomy, cell-like bedroom with bare whitewashed walls where I'd been a prisoner since that encounter on the river bank. During that time I'd had nobody to talk to. One bowl of watery soup a day was delivered by a young boy who never spoke. I knew from discussions with other God's Own Democracy victims that this was just the first stage, wearing you down through hunger, isolation and boredom. The heavy stuff came next.

'Ah, Julia,' said a voice from the far end of the room. 'Come in.'

As my eyes adjusted to the light, I focused on a portly middle-aged man in a navy blue suit. He sat on a kind of throne. I walked towards him, Charlotte holding onto my arm.

'Do sit down.'

I plonked myself on the chair opposite him.

'That will be all, Charlotte.'

'Sanctified One.'

The major began to leave. The Sanctified One addressed her again.

'Oh, Charlotte, you'll be sanctified tonight.'

She looked at him in surprise.

'But it's not my turn.'

He smiled.

'I think you should have a reward for the good work you have done.'

Now it was her turn to smile.

'Oh, thank you, Sanctified One.'

She left.

'So you're the sanctified one?' I asked.

'I have that honour. How are you, Julia?'

Confused? Distraught? Terrified?

'OK,' I said.

He smiled.

'Good, good. I just wanted to explain one or two things, give you some idea of your options.'

I put my hands on my lap, twisting them together. Biting my bottom lip, I could hear the rumble of my stomach, brought on by hunger and fear.

'Luke will be along in a moment with some tea,' he went on.

'Right.'

'You are the first person to be arrested under a law passed just last week.'

'The one that outlaws wanking.'

A flicker of anger crossed his face, then disappeared.

'God's Own Democracy has done some good work, some wonderful work.'

Oh, no, could I face a party political broadcast? Did I have a choice?

'Abortion was banned; sexual intercourse outside marriage was made illegal. So was homosexuality. Contraception too.'

'I know all this,' I said.

'Of course you do, Julia. This is just context. We thought we had all the bases covered, then you came along with your SPOMM.'

He almost spat the last word.

'The Society for the Promotion of Mutual Masturbation,' I said.

Again the flicker of anger.

'There is no need to spell it out.'

'Oh, but there is, we need to spell things out, be honest and open.'

'Not now, Julia,' he said.

'Yes, now,' I shouted. 'We promote the one way for people to achieve sexual fulfilment within the law, without risking unwanted pregnancy or disease. And we make it clear what we are talking about.'

I could have said more: no performance anxiety; no penetration means no thought of conquest; both partners get satisfaction.

'What you're advocating is against God's law.'

I shrugged. There was no point in saying any more.

'I need to make sure you understand the charges against you.'

'You'll have a job,' I said. 'This law is called The Seed Preservation Act…'

'True…'

'Correct me if I'm wrong, but the point of it is to prevent sperm being wasted, to make sure it is used only to make babies.'

'So that means,' he said, 'that masturbation denies a life. Masturbation is murder.'

'Hence MiM. However, I have no sperm.'

He waited a while before speaking. I thought I had him there.

'You will be charged with aiding and abetting.'

Always read the small print, I said to myself.

'And what will Hugh be charged with?' I asked. 'It was his seed that was wasted.'

He stared hard at me.

'Mr Franklin sacrificed himself for the greater good,' he said.

'What?'

'It was essential to build up evidence against you,' he went on, 'in order to destroy your organisation. Mr Franklin will not be charged with any offence. He was doing God's work.'

I heard a door open.

'Ah, here's Luke with the tea.'

I looked behind me at a man in a jumpsuit carrying a tray. At first glance he looked like an identikit G.O.D. henchman, his hair newly cut. He placed the tea things carefully on a table.

'Thank you, Luke. Just leave it there.'

'Sanctified One,' said the man referred to as Luke with a respectful intonation and a little bow.

As he walked past me on his way out, our eyes met for a second and he winked at me. I looked down at the teapot, hardly able to believe my eyes. Hoping Sanctified wouldn't see the shock on my face, I spent the next half minute pouring tea and handing him a cup.

'Now for your options,' he said. 'The first one is to stand trial, probably next week.'

I knew what that would mean. My stomach muscles tightened involuntarily, as the fear really kicked in. Sweat prickled the back of my neck and my hands shook. I had to think of something fast. The only problem was I couldn't think of a damn thing.

'You will undoubtedly be found guilty and sentenced to death.'

I'm too young to die, I said to myself, wishing I could have come up with something more profound.

'Option number two,' Hugh continued as if going through a menu, 'is for you to recant and become a nun.'

He allowed a little smirk to pass over his face.

'I'm not sure it's quite you, Julia.'

He was enjoying this, the bastard.

'Your final option is to do what Charlotte did.'

'What Charlotte did?'

This was getting beyond me. I looked out of the window to my left. I could see the tops of the trees and open countryside in the distance. Was this to be my last glance at the beauty of Lovendale?

'She was charged with… well, the details aren't important. She saved herself by joining the vanguard of God's Own Democracy.'

I shook my head to clear the fog in my brain as he explained further.

'If you followed Charlotte's example you would be responsible for the duties you've seen her carry out.'

I swallowed hard, trying to get some moisture in my mouth. What did he mean? Was I to become a turncoat? Do the dirty on my principles? A great punishment, I had to admit.

'It would also involve regular sanctification sessions.'

'Sanctification se…?'

Oh, I get it, I said under my breath, you fucking hypocrite. Would I be strong enough to say no?

'What is it with you guys?' I asked. 'You organize things so you can do what you want. Why does freedom for others bother you so much?'

'We offer the people true freedom, freedom from sin.'

I sighed as he went through the options again.

'Before you make up your mind, I'll let you talk in private with Charlotte.'

With that he left. For a couple of minutes I waited, walking aimlessly round the room, wondering if this were some elaborate trap.

'Hi, Julia,' said Charlotte as she came in.

'Hello.'

She sat down.

'The sanctified one says you want to know about joining the vanguard.'

'Er…'

She pulled a phone from the top pocket of her uniform.

'Luke,' she said, 'Julia says yes.'

'Just a minute…' I said.

Putting the phone away, she put her finger to her lips.

'Shh.'

The door opened.

'Here's Luke now,' said Charlotte.

'Ralph,' I said, 'what's happening?'

I knew as soon as I saw him that 'Luke' was Ralph but hadn't dared say anything. Two men I'd loved had betrayed me. The wink was the final insult. 'I've joined the enemy and I don't care', it seemed to say. Charlotte replied to my question.

'We'll explain later. For now, you have to do exactly as I say.'

'Like hell, I will...'

'We gotta get out of here,' Charlotte snapped back, 'unless you want us all to get killed.'

I followed them out of the room. What else could I do? We went into a large windswept field. Ralph pointed to a square, brick building on the far side of the field with a G.O.D. helicopter parked outside, its rotors spinning.

'We're heading for the VWQ, Vanguard Women's Quarters.'

Before I knew it we had reached the Vanguard building. Three women who looked like clones of Charlotte ran towards us. Then a voice spoke from behind us.

'What's going on here?'

We turned to see the colonel who was with Charlotte at the time of my arrest. Still looking spick and span in his uniform, he trained a gun on us. Shit.

'Oh, Colonel Jones,' said Charlotte. 'I am transporting the prisoner to the re-education chamber. The Sanctified One's orders.'

Amid the combined noise of the wind and the helicopter the tension that surrounded us created its own silence. Jones looked at each of us in turn. He unzipped the top pocket of his jumpsuit and took out a phone.

'I'll just check,' he said, pressing a button.

In the fraction of a second his eyes weren't on us Charlotte's boot swung out and landed between his legs. As he slumped gasping to his knees, she stepped forward. Grabbing his weapon and his phone she kneed him in the face.

'That's for all of us who had to suck your dick, arsehole,' she said as he toppled over.

The others clambered into the helicopter. I stood motionless, frozen with fear. Charlotte told me to get into the helicopter and followed me, sitting in the pilot's seat. I joined Ralph and the other three women in the seat behind her. Moments later, we were in the air.

'Could somebody please tell me what the hell's going on?' I asked.

'There's an organisation dedicated to opposing G.O.D.' said Charlotte. 'We've been working on its behalf for a year or so. Ralph's been helping us while he's been abroad.'

Guiltily I regretted the nasty thoughts I'd had about him.

'With our help he managed to infiltrate the Sanctified One's HQ,' Charlotte went on. 'We've been planning our escape. Ralph has arranged somewhere for us all to stay.'

I turned towards Ralph and we exchanged a smile, as Charlotte went on.

'We're all willing to speak openly about what's been done to us once we've left the country.'

I thought of the awkward conversation I'd had with Ralph a few weeks ago. I should have trusted him.

'We were going to leave next week, but then you were taken,' said Charlotte. 'We brought things forward.'

'Really?'

'Ralph knew we didn't have much time to save you. That guy really loves you.'

That did it. I bust into tears. Everything I'd been holding back came flooding out.

'I'm sorry, Ralph,' I managed to say between sobs. 'About everything.'

'So am I.'

Charlotte explained further.

'We're heading for Amsterdam. Friends and supporters will take us to their homes. The vanguard women will speak at a press conference today about their sexual enslavement by the Leaders of God's Own Democracy.'

'Will it do any good?'

'The UK is still a parliamentary democracy. G.O.D. won't be in power forever. We have to believe that. What comes out in the press conference will count against them at the next election.'

She raised a clenched fist.

'In the meantime, we carry on the fight.'

Money Bank

BETHANY RIDLEY-DUFF

Margi stirs the pond water with a stick, rain dripping down the neck of her dress. Above her, the willow fronds whisper against one another – a murmur of wet leaves, mostly, rising to a hiss when the wind cleaves through them. She keeps hearing her name on the breeze.

A stone plops into the pond, tossed out from behind her, and she jumps.

'Lucky I didn't push you in,' a voice calls.

Margi turns. Behind her, Lillian is almost a stranger, her face bonier, her hair shorn, her clothes too skimpy for the hammering rain. Margi grasps for something – anything – that makes her familiar, but there are only tattoos, chapped lips, nails bitten to stumps – details that slide through her grip like scree.

It's good to see you, Margi signs.

Lillian trains her eyes on Margi's hands, her face hardening. 'Seriously? You're going to do that with me?'

Margi's fingers fumble around the next signs. *It's just – anyone could hear me out here.*

Lillian says nothing for a moment, but then moves to the pond edge and slumps down on the wet concrete, drawing her knees beneath her chin the same way she did as a young child. She scoops up a handful of gravel and starts flicking it into the water.

'What do you want?' she says, not meeting Margi's eyes.

Margi bites the inside of her lip, which is already chewed ragged. *Mum's found me a match.*

Lillian stops. Then flicks another piece of gravel. 'What's that got to do with me?'

Margi's stomach knots. *Can you help me?*

A snort. 'Wow.'

Please, Margi signs. *I know I don't deserve it, but if you can just help me get–*

Lillian slaps Margi's hands, knocking the words out of the air. She heaves herself to her feet, dusts her palms and starts to walk. Margi scrambles after her, grabbing at her jacket, but Lillian shoves her off.

'Please,' Margi chokes out, her eyes burning.

Lillian looks back at her, her eyes skimming Margi's skin like the tip of a knife.

'Careful,' is all she says. 'Anyone could hear you out here.'

And then she's gone, lost to the rain.

When Lillian was nine and Margi five, they'd both had long hair. Lillian's was thick and reddish, beautiful against the pallor of her skin. Their mother would always cut it for her, brushing the feathery snippets away with her fingers then plaiting it in a long rope down her back.

You'll make a very pretty bride, she'd signed.

Then her eyes had moved to Margi, for one heavy moment, and moved away again.

She'd left the scissors on a low shelf in the kitchen, and it didn't take much for Margi to reach them – a stool and a bit of scrambling. Harder was creeping into Lillian's bedroom in the dark, feeling her way towards her bedside, sliding the blades around the thick wad of plait. It cut through almost too easily. Lillian didn't even wake up.

As Margi creeps through the front door, she listens hard, her dress dripping onto the kitchen tiles. Silence, except for the gurgle of the pipes. She crosses the floor with slow, heel-to-toe steps, edging into the hall, past the dining room, towards the stairs–

Her mother sits on the fifth step, legs planted either side of her like pillars. Margi stops.

You said you were staying in this morning, her mother signs.

Margi swallows. *I wanted to go for a walk.*

In this?

As if on cue, the wind throws a volley of raindrops against the window. Her mother's rheumy eyes don't blink. When Margi was a very young child – young enough that Lillian still lived with them, young enough that they all spoke aloud to each other – her mother used to poke her between the eyebrows when she lied, claiming she could peer right into her head and see the truth flapping to get out. Margi wonders now if she ever lost the art – if she can see Lillian's name fluttering against the inside of her skull like a moth.

I just – got nervous, Margi signs. *About Friday. I felt better when I got some air.*

Her mother's lips tighten. *You're not going to show me up, are you?*

Margi shakes her head, blood beating in her eyelids. Her mother watches her for another moment, then heaves herself to her feet. She clambers down the staircase on stiff, unoiled-clockwork legs, her face contorted. When Margi holds out a hand, she bats it away like an insect.

Get ready for church, her mother signs, easing herself down onto the landing. *He'll be there, so make yourself presentable.*

Margi nods. When she climbs the stairs, the landing mirror is waiting for her. The girl behind the glass is doughy-faced and plump, her skin still red with cold. Plain but inoffensive. Margi touches her fingertip to the girl's, wishing she was uglier.

Lillian took her vow of silence when she was ten, dressed in the heavy blue silks that their mother had worn for her own ceremony. Like most things, they suited her, and her face stayed clear and calm beneath the mesh veil. She didn't duck her head as the priest called out the conditions, nor did her hands shake as she carved her pledge into the air, offering her voice up to God.

Margi had been too plump for the silks by her own ceremony, but she'd worn them anyway, sweating into the sleeves. Her hands fumbled over the pledge, fingers stiff and cumbersome. All the way through, her tongue itched in her mouth as if it had something to say.

At church, they sit in the leftward gallery with the rest of the pledged women. Margi fidgets between her mother's baton arms and the spiked elbows of Mrs Penstack, who keeps her chin in the air. She used to teach Margi the piano, but she hasn't spoken to her for over four years, not since Lillian–

Margi forces the thought away.

She's supposed to keep her eyes forward throughout the service, but she can't stop them from sliding to the right during the prayers, blurring on the gallery where the men and children stand. He's in there somewhere, she thinks mistily. She's seen him twice before, but she doesn't trust her memory of him. His body balloons in her mind's eye, his skin wrinkling like leather, his face twisting into gargoyle features.

Her mother's nails dig into her palm, pulling her eyes downward again. Prayers. Focus on the prayers. Find something to pray about, something you're allowed to ask for…

At the end of the service, Margi and her mother are some of the first to leave. They pass him as they file down the aisle, and he smiles at them both, jaunting a hand. The light filtering through the church windows brings out the silver in his hair.

Margi thinks of that waving hand. Imagines it touching her.

She stops thinking about it.

At fourteen, it was decided that Lillian would marry a friend of their father's. He worked at the local practice and owned a vast, teeth-white house on the other side of the village, which was festooned in creeper and shrouded by pines. The family had visited for supper twice. Margi, not quite ten, could vaguely remember sweeping hallways and leaded windows and a chandelier like clustered raindrops. She thought of Lillian lounging beneath it, sprawled catlike across a velvet sofa, and jealousy pressed into her gut.

Her mother bought dresses, veils, bridesmaid gowns. Invitations flurried out to relatives across the world.

It was around that time that Lillian started going for walks in the evenings.

Margi cannot sleep.

Her legs fidget. Her tongue is sandpaper. Her brain is a broken, skipping record, stuttering on Lillian, then him, then Lillian, then him. He jaunts his hand at her, again and again. Lillian looks at her, again and again. Sometimes her hair is shorn, as it was in the park. Sometimes it is long, greasy at the roots, pulled back into a ponytail that says *no time, there's no time,* and she has her hand on Margi's arm and she's using her mouth to say 'trust me' and–

A clock chimes, jerking Margi from the shallows of sleep. The world takes a moment to settle into place – blackness, then shapes, then shelves and drawers and one leering wardrobe. Moonlight drips through a chink in the curtains, spilling over the clock on her bedside table. It shows midnight.

Tomorrow, she will be married.

The thought tolls in her head like the clock chimes. She feels dizzy.

She doesn't remember getting up. The record skips, and she's on her feet. It skips again, and her arms are working a jumper over her head. Again, and she's in the hall. Again. The door. Again. Again.

Four weeks before Lillian's wedding, she sat straight-backed at the dressing table in their bedroom, wrestling her curls into the beginnings of a bun. Her nape was as white as the walls.

Margi looked up from her bed. *What's that on your neck?*

There was a purple blotch nestled in the crook of her collarbone, just visible in the mirror, and Lillian flinched when she saw it. She dropped her hands at once, letting her hair spill back over her shoulders.

Must've bruised myself, she signed.

She smoothed her hair back into place, hands fidgety, then pushed back from the chair. She had something else to do now, she said.

For the second time that week, Margi finds herself kneeling by the pond, stirring her bitten nails through the black water. The sky is empty above her, the wind faded to nothing, the entire park cavernously deserted. Even God feels further away. Perhaps the moon, fat and white above the trees, has eclipsed His eye.

'Margi? What the hell's going on?'

Margi turns to see Lillian again, looking softer and younger than she did in the daylight. Her hair is rumpled, her face slack with tiredness, a ratty fleece wrapped around her shoulders. At the sight of her, something in Margi's chest splinters and breaks.

'I didn't think you'd come,' she whispers.

'Are you joking? After a call like that?'

There was a telephone box on the way to the park, litter-strewn and smelling of piss. Margi garbled something into the mouthpiece about *theparktheparkthepark* and *pleasecomeIneedyoutocome,* then dropped the phone before Lillian could say anything.

'I thought you were *hurt*,' Lillian snaps, looking Margi up and down. 'What were you playing at?'

Margi feels tears spill. 'I'm sorry.'

'You bloody should be, dragging me all the way out here. I've got *work*.'

'No, I'm *sorry*,' Margi says, starting to sob. 'I can't stop thinking about – I was so stupid.'

She can't heave any more words out. She just cries, her face slippery and hot, the world melting together around her. The gravel crunches as Lillian sits down at her side.

'Yeah, you were,' Lillian says softly. 'No use crying over it, though.'

'I didn't know she'd throw you out,' Margi wails. 'I just – I didn't–'

The words disintegrate in her mouth, but the memories crowd close. Roiling jealousy, and a thought unfolding like a scrap of paper: *Mum would be so pleased with me.* Margi presses the heels of her hands to her eyes.

'Who's Mum picked for you?' Lillian asks.

Margi doesn't take her hands away. 'Someone from church.'

'Lives nearby, then?'

Margi nods. 'So I can still come back and look after her,' she says. 'Not that she lets me, even though her arthritis is so awful now. It's been worse since Dad–'

She stops, realising that Lillian might not even know – who would tell her, when her own mother has brushed her off like dead skin? The clench in Lillian's jaw says no, she didn't know, but she does now. The moment passes.

'When do you marry him?' Lillian asks, eyes on the pond.

'Friday,' Margi says. 'Tomorrow.' A hollowness stretches through her chest. 'Lil, please–'

'No,' Lillian says. 'I can't afford to look after you.'

'You don't have to, I promise,' Margi says, crying again. 'I'll do anything. I'll sleep on the floor–'

'*No*,' Lillian snaps. 'It's not – I wish I could, okay? But it'd be worse with me. The stuff I've got to do to just – to just get by – I'm not dragging you into it.'

Margi swallows. 'Then what do I do?'

'You stick it out,' she says. 'You keep your head down and you get on with it.'

The words hit like cold water. She remembers the greasy-haired Lillian from four years ago, the one who squeezed Margi's hands and said 'trust me' with her mouth.

'You said getting away was the most important thing,' Margi says.

'Yeah, well, look where that got me,' Lillian says. 'Look, sometimes you've got to – it's not all about doing big stuff. Sometimes you've just got to bide your time. There's no point kicking out if it just gets you in a worse place.'

Margi says nothing. Lillian wraps a hand around hers.

'You remember that stupid music box, the one with the missing ballerina?' she says. 'I started storing money in that when I was, what, eleven? A pound a week, bits of change, birthday money and stuff. Because I knew I'd use it someday. To get away.' She pauses. 'Seemed like a good idea at the time.'

The last part presses between Margi's ribs like a nail. When she closes her eyes, she sees her mother's hands wrenching the box away, the lid flipping open, coins chiming against the kitchen tiles.

'You should get back,' Lillian says, straightening up. 'Don't want Mum noticing you've gone.'

Margi nods. A squeeze to her shoulder, a mumble of something that might be *good luck*, and she's gone. Wind blows through the gaps in Margi's jumper. It takes a long time for her to drag herself to her feet.

Three weeks before Lillian's wedding, a hand had dabbed at Margi's cheek in her sleep, pulling her into muddy wakefulness. It took a moment for Lillian's face to swim into focus. Her hair was greasy, tucked into a messy ponytail, and her mouth was talking – actually talking, spilling words. She was saying things about going. She was saying things about trust.

What are you talking about? Margi signed, sitting up. *Go where?*

'It doesn't matter,' Lillian whispered. 'Just need to get away. Michael says there's a place in—'

Michael?

Even in the dark, there was no missing the colour in Lillian's cheeks. 'He's been helping me. We've talked about—'

You talked to a boy? Margi signed, her heart thumping. Her brain brushed against the memory from a week ago: the purple bruise on Lillian's neck, the way she'd pulled her hair over it. *Are you mad? You're getting married soon!*

'I'm not,' Lillian said, her voice low. 'You can be bloody sure of that.'

Then everything was rushed. She was bundling Margi from her bed, fingers digging right into her shoulders, pressing her down to the floor and telling her to pack, to pack quickly, to pack *right now*. Several of Margi's dresses were already laid out for her – the blue one, the white one, the green one she only ever wore for church. When she picked one up to press it down into her rucksack, she could hardly feel the fabric beneath her fingers.

When Margi gets home, the kitchen windows are ablaze with yellow light – two open eyes in a shuttered and sleeping street. Her feet stop. They shift, as if considering running. Instead, she wraps her hand around the door handle.

Her mother sits at the kitchen table, looking decades older than she should. Her hair, free of its day bonnet, is white under the glaring kitchen lights, her eyes pouchy and tired. Flat against the table, her arthritic fingers twist sideways. She pushes herself upright.

Another walk? she signs.

In the gleam of the fridge, Margi sees how she looks to her – nightgown halfway up her legs, hair uncovered.

I'm sorry, Margi says. *I couldn't sleep.*

And the answer to that, of course, is to wander around half-naked in the middle of the night, her mother signs. *Where did you go?*

Just… around, Margi signs.

The slap is quick. It does not hurt, but the shock of it burns on Margi's skin.

Are you trying to shame me? her mother signs, tears sparking in her eyes. *Trying to shame me like your sister did?*

Margi shakes her head, a fullness pressing against her eyes. Her mother's mouth opens as if to say something, then closes again. She rubs her creased forehead.

Did anyone see you? she signs.

No, Margi signs.

Then go to bed. And stay there.

Lillian told Margi to meet her at the front door once she'd packed everything into her rucksack, and so passed a silent, surreal six minutes of Margi, shaky from waking so late, pushing and pressing clothes into the base of a bag. When she heaved it onto her shoulders, the straps cut into her flesh.

Her feet were silent on the carpeted landing, on the stairs. The photos on the wall looked alien in the darkness, her family warped behind the glass, their smiles full of too many teeth. When she stepped into the downstairs hall, Lillian was waiting by the kitchen door. The broken music box was tucked under her arm, her own rucksack sagging off her shoulders. She was plaiting her hair in a furtive, frenetic way, perhaps just to keep her hands busy. She stopped when she saw Margi.

'Ready?' she whispered.

Margi looked at the half-ravelled plait, suddenly aware of her own limbs, her feet on the carpet, the groan of a pipe somewhere above her.

One minute, she signed. *I need the loo.*

'Be quick, then,' Lillian said. 'And don't flush it – they'll wake up.'

Margi nodded, climbing the stairs again. Out of sight, she stood alone on the upstairs landing, her heart beating in her throat. She thought of her mother with her hands in Lillian's hair, telling her she'd be a beautiful bride, then of her own hands around the cumbersome scissors. The soft scrape of Lillian's plait falling away. The sting of the slap when their mother found out.

Then there was a thought, unfolding in her head like a scrap of paper. *Mum would be so pleased with me if I told her about this.*

Her eyes moved to her parents' bedroom door.
One step. Two steps.
Her arm shook as she lifted it. She knocked three times.

The morning is bright but misty, and the church smells of damp stones beneath the tang of incense. Against her arms, the wedding silk is heavy, and the veil tickles her nose and mouth when she breathes in.

Through it, her betrothed's face is softened to a blur – just a moon of creamy skin, the impression of eyes, a nose, a smiling mouth. Today, his hair looks darker, but not by much. His hands are damp on hers, and she wonders, briefly, what on earth he could have to be nervous about.

When he takes his hands away to lift her veil, her brain bumps once more against the idea of running. Lillian doesn't know everything, she thinks.

But she doesn't move. His mouth touches hers, and his lashes scrape her skin as he shuts his eyes. She keeps hers open.

She is supposed to share everything now. When she crosses the threshold into his house – *her* house – she casts a glance over the olive carpet and the ugly art on the walls, wondering if any of it could ever feel like it belonged to her. Her husband gives her a damp smile.

'That's an original piece, that one,' he says, pointing to a splotchy portrait above the shoe rack. 'Do you like it?'

Her hands move to sign something, but he catches her fingers and holds them still.

'Hey, we're married now,' he says. 'You can use your voice with me.'

She feels her throat closing. His grip on her fingers is only light, so she pulls her hands free.

It still feels strange, she signs.

He nods, almost too eagerly. 'I understand that. We can wait until – well, until you feel more comfortable.'

There are other things he claims to be willing to wait for, as well. She sleeps alone that night, in a narrow bed usually set aside for guests. The room smells musty, and the clock on the wall refuses to hang straight. She watches the second hand inch round and round and round the face, chipping away at her adjustment time, at his patience. How many days will it take until she is 'comfortable' enough for his liking?

Sleep is at low tide, too weak to sweep her away. At half past midnight, she climbs from her cold bed and sits against the wall, the plaster pressing against the bones in her spine. She passes the time by tracing her fingers over the bottom shelves of a crowded bookcase, which is strewn with notepads and Sellotape reels and pots of elastic bands. On the lowest shelf, she finds a metal money bank in the shape of a treasure chest, which is silent when she shakes it.

She holds the money bank in her lap for a few moments, watching moonlight glance off the metal. Her hand moves back to the shelves. In one pot, she finds a discoloured twenty pence.

She encloses it in her fist. Lillian's voice comes back to her.

Sometimes you've just got to bide your time.

She presses the coin into the money bank. The clink is clear in the silence.

Outside, a bird calls, and a siren squalls far in the distance. She climbs back into bed with the bank clasped in both hands, then holds it above her for a while, tilting it back and forth so she can hear the rasp of the coin inside. There'll be more coins in a house like this. Housekeeping money that can go missing.

One day at a time, she thinks.

When she sets the money bank down on the bedside table, the metal winks at her. She almost winks back.

The Calling

MICHAEL BIRD

I'd just come home from school and I was sitting on my bed, and didn't know what to do.

I was still in my uniform, and wanted to take this off, but hadn't decided if I should stay in the house or not. Maybe I could message Layla or Marie and ask if they wanted to meet in the park or the mall. But what if they didn't wanna go? Did that mean they really really didn't wanna go, or they didn't wanna go with me? It's always hard to tell why people say no. I'm never sure if it's their problem or my problem. All I can be sure of is there is a problem somewhere.

In front of my bed was a desk and mirror. Photos of Layla, Marie, Debbie and Jed were stuck to the glass. These were pictures of us by the seaside, at a fun-fair and hiking on some mountains that weren't really mountains, just hills with snow. We were hugging, kissing and making stupid faces. I'd got rid of all the photos from over one year ago. I didn't like some of the people in those pictures. I didn't like me in those pictures. It made me think that in a year's time I would no longer like the me of now. Is this what's gonna happen? Will I always hate what I was?

I began to shout. It was a loud shout. A long shout. A single pitch. High. A new type of sound. A shout I'd never shouted before. Sort of similar to a violin playing one note without stopping. But it was rough. A little scratchy. Like the bow was pressed too close to the string.

But the shout wouldn't stop. After a few minutes, Mum knocked on the door, waited for two seconds and then walked inside. She always knocked and stormed in, without giving me time to say whether I wanted her to enter or stay out. It was kinda annoying, but it was a Mum thing and I was stuck with Mum things as long as there was a Mum around to do the things that Mum did.

'What are you up to *now*?' she asked.

I kept on shouting.

'Can you please keep it down?'

The volume didn't change.

'You're gonna give me a headache.'

I shrugged.

Without moving from my bed, I didn't stop for a further hour. A car pulled up in our drive. There was a bit of an argument downstairs, and the front door slammed. Half a minute later Dad walked into the room, still in his suit and tie from work. His face was mean. But Dad mean. Like he was angry and sad at the same time.

'I can hear you all the way down the street,' he said. 'The whole neighbourhood can hear you.'

He stepped back a little.

'Someone is bound to call the police,' he said.

'Don't scare her,' said Mum.

I kept the same pitch.

'Have you nothing to say?' he went on.

'Try being nice to her,' she said.

'We're always nice to her,' said Dad, waving a finger at me, 'and this is where nice gets us.'

A few minutes later Mum wheeled in a trolley with a television.

'We thought you'd like to watch something,' she said, 'and a bit later dinner will be ready.'

Mum put on a programme that I'd told her I liked. But I'd told her I liked it three years ago. She left the room, but I knew she was standing outside. The opening credits started and I watched the show for about twenty minutes. It was the first episode of a drama, but there were some funny parts in it. I liked the characters, though the story wasn't very new or anything. It was also hard to hear the words because I kept on shouting. The programme finished. I could've watched more episodes, but Mum came back into the room.

'Why are you doing this?' she asked.

I threw my arms in the air.

It was dinner time. Mum brought in a tray of sausages, peas and mashed potato and a glass of orange squash. She laid it down on my desk with a knife and a fork folded up in a serviette. I couldn't eat the meal or drink the squash because I kept on shouting. This worried me a bit because I didn't want to go hungry or thirsty, so I made a special effort. Putting the plate on my lap, I unwrapped the knife and fork, cut a slice of sausage and stuck this in my mouth. I found that the sound could be muffled by eating the food or swallowing the squash. But when I finished, the noise began again.

Mum came in and took the tray away.

'See,' she said. 'You can control it if you want.'

I shook my head.

'I think you're being very unreasonable,' she added.

A bit later Marie came around. She was my best friend since nursery school, and our parents knew each other. We sat together in Double History and Science. But lately she'd got very close to Ada and Lillian. I found Ada and Lillian a little stuck-up, so I didn't see so much of Marie any more, except when we went out with our parents. This wasn't very often, because we didn't wanna spend evenings and weekends with our parents. It was like going out with our past. I was closer to Layla. We sat together in English and French. But my parents didn't know Layla or Layla's parents.

'Alright Ellen?'

I didn't respond.

'What's with all the *raa raa*?'

I shrugged.

'Are you sick?'

I gave no reply.

'It's kinda odd.'

She looked at the photos on the mirror.

'Your hair was so different.'

After glancing over my books, she saw my cupboard was open. Flicking through the clothes hanging up, she pulled out a tight fitting T-shirt showing a cartoon skull of a kitten with a red bow.

'Oh, I totally adore this,' she said, holding it up against her chest. 'Can I steal it for a week?'

I nodded.

'Thanks a billion.'

Mum walked into the room.

'Can you make her stop?' she asked Marie.

'I can't do what I can't do, Mrs Johnson.'

'But you're her friend.'

'Friends aren't like amazing at everything.'

'Can't you play with her?'

Marie scowled.

'Play with her?'

'You know what I mean.'

'I dunno,' said Marie. 'I got a lot on right now, and this is a bit too much.'

Two hours later. Nine in the evening. The doctor was shining a metal instrument with a tiny light into my eyes. The noise continued.

'Did anything happen today?' he asked Mum.

'She got up. She had breakfast. I drove her to school. She went to school. I picked her up. I drove her back. I went out shopping. I returned and she was doing this.'

'She didn't mention anything?'

'No,' said Mum.

'Did she play sport?'

'Not on Tuesdays.'

'And she didn't engage in any physical activity?'

'Not that I know of.'

'No bruises in the last few days? No head injuries?'

'Nothing.'

The doctor put on a loud and patronising voice as he spoke to me.

'Open wide.'

Sticking a small piece of wood on my tongue, he looked inside my mouth. The sound changed to a lower pitch for a few seconds. He jammed the buds of a stethoscope into his ears, and listened to my back and chest.

'Your throat is fine,' he said. 'Your lungs are fine. Your heart is fine.'

The doctor packed away his instruments in a leather bag and sat next to me on the bed.

'Mrs Johnson, I will have to ask you to leave this room.'

'Why?'

'I need to make a private consultation.'

Slowly, Mum closed the door behind her. The doctor stayed on the bed, but not too near to me.

'Ellen,' he said. 'I want you to reply to my questions by either nodding or shaking your head.'

I nodded.

'Good,' he said. 'You're aware that I am a doctor. A doctor isn't allowed to share people's secrets with anyone else. If he or she did, then no one would trust that doctor anymore.'

I nodded.

'When we are young, we get up to all kinds of things. Sometimes we don't tell our parents about these things. Often this is not because there is anything wrong with them, but we think it is best for our parents not to know.'

He paused.

'Have you been in any kind of accident in the last few days?'

I shook my head.

'Did you take anything recently?'

I wasn't sure what he meant.

'A pill?'

I shook my head.

'Some powder or dust?'

I shook my head again.

'A puff of smoke?'

I'd had a few cigarettes with Layla on Wednesday after school at the back of the youth club. But they were only cigarettes. The ones that kill you. Not drugs. I shook my head.

'Have you touched a boy?'

I shook my head.

'Or parts of a boy?'

I shook my head a lot.

'You can tell me, I'm a doctor.'

He looked at me for about ten seconds, like he was trying to read my face. But I knew me. There was nothing for him there.

The doctor shouted, but not too loud.

'Mrs Johnson – you can come in now!'

A few seconds later, Mum returned. I knew she'd been listening at the door.

'Why is she doing this?' she asked.
'There is no medical reason.'
'But she won't stop.'
'Try talking to her.'
'Talk? *Talk?*' said Mum. 'That's *all* we do.'

It was nearly ten o'clock. I was getting tired. The big noise was wearing me down. Like a punch, punch, punch to my throat.

A quick knock, the door opened and Mum brought in a woman who was kinda old, but not dead-old. She had long curly white hair, heavy make-up and was dressed in a flowery skirt and a tired brown shirt with sequins. Mum said this was Cecilia.

The first thing Cecilia did was smile and tell me how much she was looking forward to getting to know me. I wasn't sure why she was there and I didn't have an opinion on whether I wanted to meet Cecilia or not, but I couldn't say anything to her because I kept on shouting.

'This is a very nice room,' she said. 'Very cosy.'

She looked around and at the mirror.

'I see you have lots of friends. That's nice. Maybe you can tell me about them some day.'

She pointed to a poster behind my bed. It was a night scene with a silhouette of some gravestones, a large moon and, in gothic letters, the name of a band I sort of thought were sort of okay.

'Oh you like music,' she said. 'How lovely. I like music too. Maybe not the same things as you. But it's something I'm passionate about... oh... what a lot of books... I see you're a keen reader.'

The pitch remained the same. The volume still loud.

Gesturing to a small chair next to my computer, Cecilia asked if she could sit down. I nodded.

'Your Mum and Dad seem nice.'

I shrugged.

'But I know how parents can be. I'm a Mum. I know how I can be. I know my daughter doesn't always like her Mum.'

I didn't respond.

'I talk to a lot of young people and they tell me it's hard to find someone to listen to them. They often want to say something, but feel too embarrassed to have to say it out in the open.'

I let her speak. It seemed like she wanted to.

'But I tell them there is nothing worth keeping inside. It doesn't matter how horrible, how bad or how dirty that feeling is.'

From my desk, Cecilia picked up a ball-point pen and a piece of paper, and handed these over to me.

'Maybe you would like to write down something. Anything you want. I won't show it to your Mum. I won't look while you write. I'll only read it if you give me permission.'

I took the pen and paper and scribbled a few words. Cecilia turned away like she was playing some kinda stupid game.

A pause.

'Am I allowed to see?' she asked.

I kept on shouting.

I handed her the note.

It read:

'There's nothing I want to tell you.'

She gave the piece of paper back to me.

'But you can. Anytime.'

I wrote down:

'Yeah'

Below I added this:

'!'

For emphasis.

It was past eleven o'clock. Mum brought me a mug of cocoa and two biscuits. I ate the biscuits and drank the cocoa. They helped muffle the sound for a few moments. Then I went to the bathroom. I shouted while I sat on the toilet. I shouted in the shower. I kinda shouted at the same time as cleaning my teeth, which was a bit more difficult, but wasn't impossible. It was more of a low moan.

I went to bed and in less than a minute I was asleep. When I woke up, I started shouting again. Mum brought in a cup of tea and some bran flakes. I shouted into the tea and the cereal. I could just about eat them, although I spat out quite a lot of the milk on the floor.

I was bored in the house. I tried watching some TV, but the programmes on during the daytime were so old. They looked old, showed old stuff and they talked in that way we speak to old people. Slow and clear. Like the world was going deaf. I thought about trying the streaming service, but there were too many things to watch, and I didn't really know what I was looking for.

Messing around on my computer, I flicked though a few websites and checked my email. But after about twenty minutes, there wasn't much else to do on the net. I messaged a few friends. I told them I couldn't come to school because I was making this big noise. But I had to wait till they were out of their lessons before they could get back to me. I tried reading a couple of books, but reading books on a weekday was like being at school.

It was around noon. Under the shouting, I heard the sound of voices from the front porch. Mum was answering the door.

'I wanna see how Ellen is.'

'And you are?'

'Layla.'

'I haven't heard about you.'

'Like Ellen tells you everything.'

'Shouldn't you be at class?'

'It's lunch. I told the teachers and stuff. They said it was okay if I came to see Ellen.'

'Well, can you make her stop what she's doing?'

'I dunno.'

A few seconds later Layla came into the room. I nodded to say hello and she nodded back.

'I spoke to Gary. He says that Friday is fifty to eighty per cent on. If you wanna go to his place. His parents are gonna be out all night. He has some stuff. So it might be okay. Gary's not so bad. But I don't like his mates. I know you also think they are kinda like fucking bullshit, so if you don't wanna go, it's fine. Maybe we can convince it to be just Gary and not his mates as well. Gary might like that. He might like to be like with only two girls and no mates. But if you're still screamy, then I guess we'll call it off. Maybe it'll happen another time. You don't have to answer absolutely yes right now.'

I didn't reply.

'Can I get you anything?'

I shook my head.

Layla looked at me without talking for a few seconds.

'It's cool. But it's also crazy. Not good crazy. Crazy crazy. Crazy like I don't know what the fuck.'

I shrugged.

'So I guess I'll see you around.'

I nodded. Layla got up and left the room. Mum was standing at my bedroom door.

'Can you make her stop?' she said.

'I told you earlier,' said Layla, 'I dunno.'

'Can't you try?'

Layla gave a big sigh.

'Why?' she said.

The next day I heard some strange sounds outside our house, so I went to the window. Parked in our driveway were white vans with satellite dishes and long cables. Large men in vests were walking around with big television cameras, pointing down the street and at my window. Some TV presenters in smart clothes were talking to our neighbours.

Mum came in with some cereal and tea.

'You see all that?'

I nodded.

'You have a very important guest coming around later,' she said. 'You have to be dressed up nicely.'

I shrugged.

While I ate breakfast, I surfed the net. There was a news report with a picture of my house. Further down was a really shitty photo of me, with long hair and a bad fringe. It was from two years ago, and I was in the uniform of lower school, so I looked like a tiny little kid.

The story said that there was this girl who couldn't stop shouting. The reporter talked to some doctor who said this was a mental case, and to a psychiatrist who called this a totally new 'malady'. At the end, the report said the authorities were now 'taking an interest'. I began to sweat. I felt dizzy in the stomach. Loads of other news repeated this stuff – and they all used the same lame picture from lower school. I was angry like majorly angry with the net. I wanted to argue with the story. Tell them how wrong they were.

I turned off my computer and watched TV, switching to some channel that had programmes about people cooking things or going places. It was boring. But it was better than seeing that fuck-bad photo of me.

Four o'clock in the afternoon. More TV crews outside. The door opened. A tall man came into my room. It was someone I knew from the news. I think it was the mayor. Thinner in person, with more wrinkles on his face, he was wearing a clean and expensive suit, though it was a bit too shiny. Behind him were two tough-looking guys, also in posh suits. They stood a few steps in the rear, watching me and the window. Mum moved into the room. She brought in a bottle of water and four glasses and laid these down next to the mayor. He said thank you and Mum shuffled outside, closing the door behind her.

'Hello Ellen,' said the man. 'I'm not sure if you know who I am.'
I nodded.
'That's great. Your situation has become a matter of great importance. It's so big that even people who you don't know care about you. And all of them are wondering whether any of us can help.'
I didn't reply.
'We all want to bring you out of this situation.'
I said nothing.
'That's why we're here.'
The noise continued.
'In my job, I meet different kinds of people. Some are rich and some are poor, some are spoilt and some are vulnerable. Sometimes I can assist them and sometimes I can't. But at least they know that there is someone who can understand their problems. That's what I have come here to offer you today. Let me understand, and then I can help you.'

I leaned over and poured myself a glass of water. As I was knocking it back, the noise went away. I looked at the mayor. The corners of his mouth perked up. His eyes flashed. He looked left to one of the guys in a suit, as if responding to a signal.

I finished the water. My throat was clear. I put down the glass. I began to shout again.

Two days later, Mum led me down to the basement. It was warm and cosy, but the air was a little stifling and there was no daylight. In the last couple of years it had become a spare bedroom for anyone coming to visit who didn't care too much about where they slept.

But something had changed. The walls and the ceiling of the room were covered in grey foam with little peaks, like some weird carpet. Mum had also put a few framed photos of my friends on the bedside table.

'Your Dad and I will bring the rest of your things,' she said.

I nodded.

'I'm sure it won't be for long.'

I could've done with a cigarette. But my parents didn't know I smoked. I couldn't get Layla to smuggle one in because Mum and Dad would smell it and then they might not let Layla come back again. It was alright when Layla came around. She told me about stuff. She was going steady with Gary right now. She didn't like him much. I wasn't crazy keen on him. But she said it was better to go out with Gary than not to go out with Gary.

When the food came, for a few minutes there was not much noise. I didn't eat a lot because Mum always gave me too much. When I finished, I felt sort of satisfied. Then Mum took away my plate and I started shouting again.

There was no interruption from outside. I could hear nothing else but me. It became so familiar. It was like listening to the lawn or the pavement. The sound of zero. I hadn't minded it for days now. I knew I would never mind the cry.

About the Authors

Mary Fox is a qualified chemical engineer, of Irish parentage, from Tooting, South London who now works as a maths and English tutor in Epsom. She shares her home with her Iraqi husband, two children and a couple of hens named Pepsi and Shirley. She started writing four years ago and has been shortlisted and highly commended in a number of short story competitions including *Surrey Life* magazine, Fish, Grist and Winchester Writers' Festival.

Martin Nathan worked variously as a labourer, showman, pancake chef, fire technician, train engineer and signal engineer on the London Underground after time at medical college. His writing concentrates on the horror of the everyday: uncovering the dark forces that operate in familiar worlds. He has won prizes and been shortlisted in Bristol Short Story, Grist, The Short Story prize, CroMagnon, Women in Comedy, Fish and been published by Tangent Press, Hissacs, Here Comes Everyone and Grist's *Experiments in Points of View*. He is one of the writers contributing monologues to the Young Vic 'My England' project. His novel *A Place of Safety* is published by Salt Publishing. He is currently studying for an MA in Creative Writing at Birkbeck College.

M. A. Hodgson moved to Huddersfield in 2009, following successful careers in book publishing and national newspapers, and started a copywriting business. Michelle is the Festival Director of the award-winning Huddersfield Literature Festival (hence sending in her entry for Grist under a pseudonym) and is currently working on a novel.

Bruce Harris began writing in 2004 after a career in teaching and educational research. To date, he has published four short fiction collections, the first two consisting entirely of stories which have won prizes, commendations or listings in U.K. competitions. He has also published two anthologies, including published and award-winning poems. A new collection of 'rites of passage' fiction, *Fallen Eagles*, will be published in 2019, as will another poetry anthology, *The Huntington Hydra*. Following his partner's diagnosis of Huntington's Disease, an inherited illness involving deteriorating physical and cognitive problems, in October 2016, he is donating his takings from his writing to Huntington's Disease charities. See www.bruceleonardharris.com for publication and awards lists, and sample writing.

Bex O'Gorman is currently in the third year of a Ph.D. in Creative Writing at UoH. She can also be found assisting with the teaching on a number of Creative Writing modules. Her research is based around the shrouded subject of rent boys in Victorian London and how the reticence surrounding child abuse has evolved. She is looking to publish her debut novel at the end of her Doctorate.

Ledlowe Guthrie worked as Sheffield editor for *State of the Arts* national magazine but now teaches writing and records oral histories at a hospice in Sheffield. She has an MA with Distinction from Sheffield Hallam and is *still* working on her first short story collection.

Tabitha Bast lives with a child and a cat in a cooperative community in inner-city Leeds, undertaking an Ms.C. in psychosexual therapy. With writings ranging from political articles to fictional short stories, previous work includes *Eclectica Magazine*, *Plan C*, and Novara Media online, and in print *Shift*, *Dysophia*, and a chapter in the book *Occupy Everything*. Tabitha was also longlisted for the Walter Swann Short story Prize and received honourable mention with the Literary Taxidermy Short Story Competition 2018.

Miriam Burke has had stories published in anthologies and magazines and a number of her stories won awards. She is from the West of Ireland and lives in London.

Elizabeth Woodgate has worked in teaching and literature development and is now a full time writer, based in Shaftesbury, Dorset. She has been published in *Mslexia*, *The Housman Anthology* and was commissioned to write an audio story walk for the Basingstoke Literary Festival. Recently, she has written a monologue for the Shaftesbury Fringe in the voice of an elderly, sixteenth century nun, who is losing her home during the dissolution of Shaftesbury Abbey. Elizabeth is currently writing her second novel and has a story coming out in the first anthology from Little Red Writers, a publishing company based in Poole, Dorset.

Jonathan Holland was born in Macclesfield and now lives in Spain, working as a teacher and as a film journalist. A former student on the Creative Writing course at the University of East Anglia, he has recently returned to writing fiction after a too-long layoff, having at the end of the last millennium published a novel, *The Escape Artist*, and several stories. He is currently working on a story collection.

A. B. G. Murray The artist formerly known as genderfluid fake celebrity Vienna Famous. Doting Dad, tree kisser, flower sniffer, soft lad. Unicorn/fawn. Given to inappropriate giggling. Shy extrovert or something. Gender denier. Body Dysmorphic freak. Prince William lookabitlike. Pop culture prosumer. Journalist for *Artrocker* and *Flux* et al., features/interviews with Johnny Rotten, Jarvis Cocker, Jon Ronson, Arthur Brown, Zoe Pilger. Fiction publications: as Vienna Famous, *Plankton* (Galley Beggar Press, 2013); as Alex Murray, *A Haunting* (Grist, 2019); Writer & illustrator, *Shame Hunters* (*Sheffield* anthology, Dostoyevsky Wannabe, 2019). Awards: Winner (Virago Prize for Essay on Women's Writing, 2003), *Sycamore Walk* (Commended; Orwell Society Dystopian Fiction Prize, 2015). Watch out for novel *Mushroom City* in the near future.

Matt Hill is an economic migrant to Bradford from London via Norfolk. Every day he cocks a snook at perfectionism. He feels he could wipe his arse better. Despite knowing there are more deserving targets for his ire, he gets angry about body hair shaming. His life goal is to grow old without growing up.

Aaron Haviland was born in America and moved to England when he was eight. He has recently graduated from the University of Huddersfield with an MA in Creative Writing. *Last of Them* is his first published story.

Sarah Hussain is a Huddersfield based author and educator. Her first novel *Escaped from Syria* was a winner finalist in the People's Book Prize Award and her short story collection *Sit up, Stand up, Speak up* was released in 2017. In 2018 she won the Ms Shakespeare competition in Yorkshire and was commissioned to write a monologue, which was performed on International Women's day. Sarah uses her writing as a means of expression and she hopes to be able to use her writing to educate and promote tolerance.

Robert Kibble has been writing for three decades now, and has been published in the magazine *Writers' Forum*, Transmundane Press, Three Drops Poetry and Exeter Writers' Flash Fiction anthology. You can find more of his burblings at www.philosophicalleopard.com wherein you could also discover his unhealthy love of zeppelins.

J. H. Lewis comes from a mixed Irish, English and Welsh working-class background, born in Leicester. He has more recently spent time in the Eastern Cape of South Africa, working with teachers on English Language projects. These experiences have been a rich source for his fiction writing. In the 1980s and '90s he became involved in the politics and the Troubles in Northern Ireland. These experiences have heavily influenced his writing. After the last Iraq war, he decided to apply for Irish citizenship and consider himself an Irish writer. Over the years he has written a range of poetry and prose. He has been published on a couple of websites and a minor American fiction publisher, and previously in Grist. He is currently working on his novel *Blueshirt,* a history of the troubles seen through the eyes of an Irish family.

He has been married too many times and has stopped now at number three. He has two estranged older children and a fantastic teenage daughter who is mercilessly critical of any pomposity he aspires to.

Bud Craig was born and bred in Salford, but has spent more than half his life in a village near Darlington. He is a member of the Crime Writers' Association (*CWA*). His books featuring Salford private investigator Gus Keane (*Tackling Death, Dead Certainty* and *Falling Foul*) are published by The Book Folks *(TBF)*. TBF have also published S*alford Murders,* the Gus Keane trilogy and *High Profile,* a collection of award winning short stories. His one act play, *The Scottish Play*, was performed at Darlington Arts Centre in 2012. More recently he has written articles for *Wooster Sauce* (the magazine of the PG Wodehouse Society) and *Red Herrings* (the CWA magazine). His next book, set in the North East of England, will be published by TBF early in 2019. When not writing Bud enjoys reading, watching cricket, cooking and walking. He also tries to keep up with his 5 grandchildren. Bud's daughter, Claire Moss, is also a published novelist.

Bethany Ridley-Duff is an undergraduate student from the University of Huddersfield, who entered the Grist contest under a pseudonym. Soon to complete her degree in English Language and Creative Writing, Beth spends most of her free time writing and consuming ungodly amounts of pizza. *Money Bank* is her second published story.

Michael Bird is a writer and narrative journalist based between Bucharest and London, looking to experiment with form, content and media, and the boundaries between fiction and non-fiction. Previous published work includes *The Two Tones of the Plait* and *England Doesn't Want You* in the Bristol Short Story Prize Anthologies, *Fallout* in Storgy's Exit Earth Anthology and *These Walls of Me* in The Short Story Net. As a journalist, he has investigated government corruption in Eastern Europe, fake news by the British media, the scourge of HIV in Europe, and home-made killer drugs in Ukraine and Georgia, and he regularly contributes as a guest correspondent to BBC Radio 5 'Up All Night'.

ABOUT GRIST

Grist offers a valuable platform for new writers. By publishing emerging writers alongside more established names, Grist offers an exciting opportunity for those starting out in their writing careers. Our writers have gone on to win prestigious awards and attract successful book deals. Find out more about us at www.hud.ac.uk/grist

ACKNOWLEDGEMENTS

With thanks to our editorial team and to our judges Helen Mort, Adelle Stripe and Kim Moore.

Special thanks are also due to Megan Taylor for her patience and good humour throughout the whole process, and to my colleague Michael Stewart for guidance and advice.

Many thanks to the University of Huddersfield Press for their continuing support.